TREE OF
PARADISE

Jane Arbor

TREE OF PARADISE

G.K.HALL&CO.
Boston, Massachusetts
1985

Published in Large Print by arrangement
with Mills & Boon Limited.

G. K. Hall Large Print Book Series.

Set in 16pt Plantin.

Library of Congress Cataloging in Publication Data

Arbor, Jane.
   Tree of paradise.

   (G. K. Hall large print book series)
   1. Large type books.   I. Title
[PR6051.R25T7   1985]   823′.914   85–5840
ISBN 0–8161–3893–1 (lg. print)

TREE OF PARADISE

CHAPTER ONE

The bustle attendant upon the arrival of an aircraft was over. The knot of people behind a rustic trellis barrier had done their waving and shouting of their greetings to the straggle of incoming passengers, who in their turn had gone through Customs and Immigration before being collected or dispersing on their own, and now the modest inter-island, one-runway airport was left to what was probably its customary afternoon stupor.

Officials, quickly divested of linen uniform jackets, strolled and gossiped in their shirt-sleeves; the Bureau de Change closed down; the last of half-a-dozen taxis, disappointed of a fare, revved up and departed; the owners of the boutiques in the duty-free annexe came out to sit in front of their gift counters and fan themselves, and the air-conditioned restaurant-cum-bar had only three customers—Donna, sitting close under the counter with her back to it, and a yard or two away, two men also turned from it, elbows rested backwards against it as they talked over their long drinks.

For the nth time since she had taken refuge

from the sizzling heat coming off the tarmac outside, Donna glanced at her watch.

Four thousand miles of Atlantic flight behind her, and Bran hadn't had the common courtesy to be on time to meet her! Her plane had been punctual and he—or Uncle Wilmot—had been airmailed as to when it was due. Yet neither of them was here, and she was going to give them just another ten minutes, or as long as it took her to finish her iced grapefruit juice, before she telephoned the Louvet Estate to demand why!

Her order had itself taken twenty minutes to be served, at the hands of the single waiter who was now making a tour of the tables, wiping them clean of non-existent stains and furnishing them with cutlery or china by making individual slow journeys to the back quarters of the restaurant for each piece he required. He moved at the rate of a walker in a slow-motion film, and as she watched his leisurely, mobile-hipped progress, something clicked in Donna's memory, a phrase forgotten from childhood until now— 'Larayan time.'

Larayan time. At eight years old, she remembered asking what it meant, to be told it was the island's kindly tolerance of unpunctuality. Mere 'time' was unexpectedly prompt time; Larayan time could be anything up to an hour of tardiness, and would still be forgiven. For who, on age-old, seasonless, tideless, all-summer Laraye, need hurry unduly? Except, perhaps, from an earthquake, a hurricane or a volcanic eruption, none of which had been more than unfulfilled threats for many years. To achieve Larayan time for any lesser urgency was, by the island's judgment, good enough.

Donna straightened her face to gravity as she saw that one of the two men had noticed the half-smile which the memory had brought to her lips. His brows had lifted, as if in question that the smile had been meant for him or his companion. So she looked away. Meanwhile she felt a little kindlier towards her cousin's or his father's delay of welcome to her. They had both lived in Laraye for so long that to all intents they *were* Larayans, with easy-going habits to match. Perhaps their car had had a puncture or they had been held up in traffic. She would give them a little longer than her threatened ten minutes.

She sipped her juice and found she was listening to the talk of the two men, having no scruples at doing so, as listening in to strangers was not eavesdropping, but mere idle interest in one's kind. Nor were they troubling to keep their voices down as they discussed local conditions and people and seemed to understand each other in unfinished sentences and meaningful shrugs or nods.

She studied them when they weren't looking her way; decided they were colleagues of a sort and that the more formally dressed of the two—wearing a jacket and collar and tie and owning a bulging briefcase—might be travelling by the next plane due, and that the other one was seeing him off.

The latter—the one who had met her smile—was the taller. His hair was reddish-brown, making a curved eave above his broad brow and a thick club-cut at his nape. His shoulders were wide and athletic-looking; his hips narrow by contrast. His clothes were those which she was to come to recognise as almost the Larayan male uniform known as the 'shirtjak'—the tailored shirt, worn open-necked and over the trousers, and of almost any hue or pattern under the sun. His eyes, Donna noticed, ranged through a whole gamut of expressions as she watched the two talk—deep interest, amusement, emphatic agreement, casual acceptance, but no boredom.

4

A pretty vibrant type, was Donna's mental verdict on him—and she realised with a sharp stab of dismay that she was no longer merely listening in. She was eavesdropping.

For she had heard a name that was familiar to her—Louvet, the title of her uncle's banana plantations. And then his name—Torrence—which was also her own. The two were discussing him and the estate in no complimentary terms and, affronted by the criticism, Donna kept straight on with her eavesdropping, feeling it was justifed in view of her involvement.

The taller man had said, 'I doubt if Louvet has turned in a decent consignment these last two years. Not that Torrence could seem to care less.'

The other man said, 'Can't the Growers' Association do something about it? Discipline him, or at worst, expel him?'

'No affair of theirs, as long as he pays his whack and goes on nominally growing a crop. While it is banana land and Torrences own it, he can let it down as he pleases.'

'Well, if he has no success with bananas, why doesn't he switch? To aubergines or pineapples or avocadoes? Or even sell out?'

'If he cared, there's no reason why he shouldn't make a go of bananas. Louvet marches alongside Marquise, and there's nothing to choose between them as to land. Anyway, he's too hidebound to switch, and too dog-in-the-manger to sell. I know, for I'd willingly add it to Marquise, and have put out feelers for it. But—' a shrug.

'You're not popular, for your success with Marquise?'

The tall man laughed. 'An understatement. I'm Genghis Khan, Attila the Hun and the original bloated plutocrat. Wilmot Torrence and I don't mix. Or not willingly.'

'Well, there's a boy, isn't there? What about him?'

'Estate-wise, he's a non-starter too. A land rock that wants to be in the water, and yearns for the shore once it gets there. Can't settle. Currently he's working for Margot le Conte as a kind of gentleman tourist guide.'

'Ah, Margot.' The other man seemed to recognise the name. He returned to his questioning. 'Why doesn't the parent company—Torrence and Son, isn't it—send out a trouble-shooter to put a bomb under the two of them, I wonder? "And Son", for instance?'

'Yes, well, they're only in Import now. With Wilmot T. they still have an interest in

6

Louvet, but after sugar failed here years ago, they sold out and went back to England to import sugar and rum, though bananas must now be their biggest deal. A sizeable slice of the land they used to own is now part of Marquise—the *best* slice, one hears, to the green in the eye of friend Wilmot Torrence! And anyway, there isn't an "and Son" to that side of the family. Just—'

Simultaneously they both looked up and listened to a far-off but gradually nearing hum from the sky. They both set down their glasses. 'That will be yours,' said the tall man. 'It's due.'

'Yes. But don't wait for take-off, please.'

'I won't either. Just see you to the departure gate.' They went out together as the airport personnel, newly dynamised by the imminent arrival of another aircraft, put on its jackets, busied itself at counters, and drove luggage-carriers out towards the runway—the whole operation being as tranquilly conducted as at a country railway station on a branch line.

Donna stayed where she was. In a minute or two she *would* go and telephone. But first she needed to collect her poise, to make sense of a mental jigsaw and to nurse her righteous gall over that obliquely petty gossip. She had

7

become aware of a counter-irritant too—a physical one. Under the thin mesh of her stocking her left ankle and calf were itching in several places; she could see and feel the telltale lumps which meant insect bites, and the impulse to scratch was almost irresistible. She compromised by rubbing her ankle with the toe of her other sandal, which made her look knock-kneed but afforded a little comfort while she pieced the jigsaw.

Marquise. Yes. The huge banana estate which neighboured small Louvet. From time to time it had figured—sourly—in her uncle's letters. As had also its owner's name—Vance, Elyot Vance—which made, didn't it, the taller one of her late companions Vance himself—the self-satisfied, opinionated cock of the walk, with his impertinent thumbnail sketches of Uncle Wilmot and her cousin Brandon, which she would bet he thought clever and dry and caustic! Well, if only he knew what *she* thought of them, uttered in public! And it didn't take much to guess that when he had broken off at the sound of the incoming plane, he had been about to say 'Just a girl'—dismissing her, Donna Susan Torrence, as a considerably lesser mortal than the non-existent 'And Son' they had seemed to find so droll.

She was almost sorry he had said that he and her uncle didn't mix. For she would have welcomed a chance to cut him down to size. How, she didn't know, but there should be ways... Meanwhile, remembering that at the moment she wasn't too pleased herself with her maligned relatives, she stood up, gathered her hand-luggage and was poised on one leg, giving her ankle a last savage massage, when Elyot Vance reappeared and came across to her, purpose in every stride.

'You're still here.' He made a statement of it, then glanced down. 'And suffering too, I see.'

'Yes, I've been bitten by mosquitoes.'

He laughed. 'You haven't read the right travel brochures. We have no mosquitoes on Laraye.'

'Well, I doubt if I'm being chewed by vampires,' Donna retorted tartly. 'Do you mind—?'

She meant the question to indicate that he was in her way. But he did not move. 'I came back because, if you were still here, I was going to offer you my services,' he said. 'That is, if you aren't camping here for the night, may I give you a lift somewhere?'

Donna said, 'Thank you. But I'm being met.'

His brows went up. 'Met? You came off the Antigua plan, didn't you? Your friends' timing isn't very good, is it?'

'I was just going to telephone to see if my uncle or my cousin could have been held up.' She fixed Elyot Vance with a cold eye. 'My uncle is Mr Wilmot Torrence of Louvet,' she said.

'Louvet?' he echoed. 'Well, well, how one's indiscretions do come home to roost! You—er—heard?'

'How could I help it? You and your friend weren't exactly whispering, were you?'

He shrugged. 'Just chatting while waiting for his take-off for Grenada. He's in the spice business. And we weren't to know a recording angel was present. If I thought about you at all, I concluded you were a rather disorientated tourist. Whereas in fact you are—?'

'Donna Torrence. The "And Son" of "the other side of the family",' she quoted.

His glance measured her slight feminine figure from head to toe. 'Really? You surprise me. How come?' he asked.

'My father is a fan of Charles Dickens.' She was gratified to puzzle him, and then wasn't so pleased when he understood what she meant. She had expected he would need to

10

have the reference explained to him, and he didn't.

'Ah—Dombey And Son who were really Dombey And Daughter? I see. Good thinking, if your father wanted a son, got a daughter instead, and made the best of the situation, as old Dombey *père* did,' he commented. 'And so you are his "And Son" partner, are you?'

'I work in the firm as his personal secretary. But I'm not a partner in it,' Donna said, wishing he hadn't summed up so acutely her father's disappointment at his lack of a son. Most people, even when they recognised it, had the delicacy to refrain from spelling it out...

'Nor a militant trouble-shooter, one imagines?' she heard Elyot Vance asking.

After his caustic criticism of her Uncle Wilmot, she wasn't going to admit that that, in a sense, was what she was. If he 'thought about' her at all, let him discover for himself the part-purpose of her coming out to Laraye! She said shortly, 'Of course not. I've come to visit my uncle and my cousin Brandon. And now, if you'll let me pass, I'm going to telephone to them.'

'There's a booth just round the corner. I'll wait to hear the result,' he offered.

11

'Please don't.'

But he was still there when she emerged from the kiosk to report that their housekeeper, Juno, had said that both Mister and Young Mister were out—Mister, she believed, gone to the library, Young Mister 'out on de job'. She had seemed surprised that Donna should believe she was expected today.

'Then that settles it. I'll have to drive you,' said Elyot Vance. 'By the way, I don't have to introduce myself? You'll have heard of me, no doubt?'

'Yes. And *from* you,' Donna added, 'that you and my uncle don't get on. So do you think he would approve your offering me a lift to Louvet?'

'The alternative being your waiting around until they do choose to remember your existence?'

'I could get a taxi.'

'Nonsense. There's no need, when our roads are the same and we're neighbours—or as near as makes for neighbourhood on Laraye. So don't quibble, and come along.' He glanced again at her purpling ankle. 'We'll stop off in the town and get you some repellent spray for any future attacks from our non-existent mosquitoes. Or no—on

12

second thoughts, we won't. It's closing day for the shops in Calvigne. Sorry, no deal.'

'That's all right.' She went with him to his car, and he put her luggage in the boot.

'We need only skirt the town; then we climb,' he said. 'I hope you're not nervous of heights, for you'll have to get used to them here. Also to mile upon mile of potholed roads at which old Macadam, the surfacing chap, would turn in his Victorian grave.' As the car took a new height he pointed. 'Look—the harbour. There's a cruise liner in—there, at the dock, do you see?'

Donna sat forward and noticed that distance and height had made the busy harbour as much of a collection of toy sheds and toy shipping as it had appeared from her incoming aircraft. 'We're driving inland and away from the sea all the time?' she asked.

'In a manner of speaking, yes. Though you'd be surprised how, owing to the turns of the coast and the long inlets and creeks, the sea is apt to turn up around the next corner, as it were. At Marquise I'm a fair distance from it, but at Louvet, being lower, you're not much more than a stone's throw from your private beach. You swim, I suppose?'

'Oh yes.' Noticing the water-filled potholes in the track and the ridged slither of red mud

13

ahead, 'It must have rained quite a lot very recently,' she remarked.

A nod. 'And that'—the car bounced into and out of a pothole and was manoeuvred expertly through the mud—'that, like the complete extinction of our mosquitoes, is something else you shouldn't take as gospel straight from the brochures' mouth—namely that, year in, year out, it's eternal, sun-filled golden days in the East Caribbean—for it's not.'

For a moment Donna was silent. Then she said, 'I know.'

'A tourist—and you're neither surprised nor affronted by the news?' he mocked.

'No. Because I remember how it used to rain. Suddenly, rather as a child cries, and stops as suddenly. And when it rains almost out of a clear sky or only from one or two clouds, there's a Larayan saying about it. I can't remember quite how it goes—'

It was his turn for silence. Meaning to surprise him, she evidently had. Then he said 'It goes: "The Devil is beating his wife again." That is, the Devil losing the fight when the sun continues to shine, and winning it when the rain persists. But how did you know?'

'I told you—I remembered. I was born on

14

Laraye,' she said.

He threw her a swift glance. 'You were? When?' He paused. 'All right, I know it's a question no gentleman asks, but you are young enough not to mind. So when?'

'Twenty–two years ago.'

'Then I beat you to it by ten years. And so—?'

'My people went back to England when I was eight. My mother had always disliked the Caribbean, and none of us has been back since.'

'Where did you live when you were here?'

'In Calvigne. But there was another house to which I used to be taken to spend the day, and sometimes, for a treat, to sleep there for a couple of nights. It was the original planter's house on the estate. It was all sugar then, of course.'

'And it's still there, on Louvet land, though exactly on the border of Marquise.' He paused. 'Well, that puts a frame round you, so here's one for me. I was born here too. My father was French descended— "Vance" is a corruption of "Voyance"; my mother was Scottish—hence Elyot. When the French owned Laraye, they were generous with their gifts of land, and my great-great-grandfather's share was Marquise, also under

15

sugar until the trade failed. Both of my parents died in the Calvigne fire which destroyed a lot of the town. But meanwhile my father had gone into banana-growing early, and since I've inherited, I've expanded a lot.'

Donna said, 'So we've heard from my uncle.'

'And if you were listening to all I was saying to my friend Grant just now, you'd have heard that I'd be willing to take over Louvet at the right price.'

'The right price as it appears to you—or to Uncle Wilmot?'

'A good question. But I'm afraid the principals haven't got as far as discussing price, owing to the door of prejudice which your respected relative keeps firmly closed.'

'Though if he doesn't want to sell, does that necessarily make him the dog in the manger you accused him of being to your friend?' Donna retorted.

'I declare, you *were* listening to future purpose, weren't you?' his tone mocked her. 'But as I understand the epithet, it means the refusal to give up, for stubbornness' sake, something you don't value yourself. So in the circumstances, I stand by "dog in the manger". What, for instance, do you know

16

about the Louvet land?'

Donna drew a sharp breath. 'I've only just arrived! How should I know anything for it or against it?'

'Sorry.' He didn't sound particularly contrite. 'What I really meant to ask was whether—news of its present condition having percolated through to Torrence And Son—you were on a mission of inspection perhaps. But that, I daresay, you could tell me is no affair of mine?'

'Yes, well—you're right,' she said.

'Right? Then you are—?'

'Right—that it's no affair of yours,' she snapped, and waited for the snub to take effect, which it did not.

He only laughed. 'Door-slamming on purposeful discussion evidently runs in your family! However, let's not press the point,' he offered. 'How long, then, are you staying—on holiday?'

She was glad of the switch of subject. For, forced on to the defensive for her uncle's management of Louvet, she would have hated him to know how shrewd had been his guess as to the reason for her open-ended errand to Laraye. She answered him indifferently, 'I don't know. It depends—' And before he could ask on what it depended, added, 'How far have we to go now? Are we nearly there?'

'Just about. Presently you'll get a glimpse of the sea again—the Anse Louvet, that will be, and then we drop down to your uncle's house.'

And drop they did—suddenly and precipitately at a V-fork off the road—down a badly ridged track leading to a wide stretch of crab grass on which Elyot Vance made a big U-turn with the car and backed it up to the side wall of the house, a long, open-verandahed bungalow which faced outward to the Anse Louvet, the tiny bay below from which it took its name.

Donna recognised the house from snapshots of it. On cold winter days in England she had often longed to experience the brooding heat from which that shadowed verandah would afford relief if you wanted it. She had pictured the grey-to-pink of tropical dawns, and sunsets over seas streaked green through blue to pure amethyst, and her imagination had heard the high chirrup of tree-frogs which, as a child, until she learned differently, she had supposed were eccentric birds which sang all night. Whenever she had thought about it, she had known an ache of memory of this island. And now she was here again. And the heat was indeed intense. And there was no one of her own to welcome her. And the verandah was shabby, with gaps in its balustrading and the paint of its woodwork cracked, and in contrast with the glare outside, the inner recesses of the house were dark as caves.

As Elyot Vance took her cases from the car and brought them to the verandah steps, a stout West Indian woman—Juno, no doubt—emerged from the shadowed interior. She wore a garish flowered overall, a jangle of bracelets on each bare forearm and a quiff of scarlet ribbon and feathers pinned to her topknot of black hair. She reached for the suitcases, but Elyot Vance eluded her and carried them into the house. As she and Donna followed him in, she stated with conviction, 'You not come today, missus. You come tomorrow. Mister say so, so I know.' And then, as if accepting the very real fact of Donna's presence, she bared magnificent teeth in a smile and added, 'But you here now. So I go, make room ready for you. Today or tomorrow—what matter?' She disappeared, humming *Old Man River* off-key as she went.

As her sight adjusted from sunglare to ordinary light, Donna looked about her.

19

There was no hall; the verandah gave directly into this room through a half wooden, half glass sliding wall. There was too much furniture of mediocre quality; the white distemper of the remaining three walls was yellowing to beige, and in an island which was rich in flowers, still nobody had troubled to arrange any here. It was obviously a room where people lived. But it had no air of being loved.

Watching her, Elyot Vance asked, 'So far—up to expectation? Or worse than? Or better?'

She guessed he was testing her reaction to the house, but, on the defensive for it, she pretended to think he meant her impressions of Laraye.

'How can I tell? I've hardly seen anything yet,' she said, and knew she hadn't deceived him when, on a short laugh, he retorted, 'And in the face of the enemy, loyalty is all, isn't it?'

'The enemy? What enemy?'

'The one that I assumed too hastily "And Son" had come out to face, and got snubbed for my pains. Of course, you're on holiday merely. So may I wish you a good welcome and good swimming and realities which don't let your memories down?'

'Thank you,' said Donna. 'And thank you for coming to my rescue. How far away do you live yourself?'

'Through the plantations, not very far. By the road, a few more twists and climbs, and my house stands high enough to afford a view over almost the whole of Marquise. How good, by the way, is your memory of the plantations?'

'None. Or very few. I told you, we left Laraye before bananas became the main crop instead of sugar. At work I've filed data on bananas, and invoiced bananas, and hunted lost consignments of bananas, and typed hundreds of letters about them—'

'And slipped on the odd banana-skin, I daresay?'

'Yes, that too,' she smiled.

'Without ever having traced a bullhead through its cycle from push-out to harvest and shipment and ripening? All that paperwork theory, and you haven't wanted to know?'

'But of course I have, and I do know the whole process in theory,' she defended herself. 'It's just that I haven't seen it in practice, and I'm sure that my uncle will rectify that while I'm here.'

'Of course,' her companion agreed

21

blandly—too evenly altogether for Donna's recollection of his out-spoken criticism of Louvet and Wilmot Torrence when he hadn't known she had overheard. But she couldn't very well pick a fresh quarrel over a mere tone of voice into which she may have read more irony than he had intended, and even surprised herself by realising that she didn't really want to quarrel with him—as long as he didn't deliberately provoke her.

She watched him as he left her to go back to his car; liked his athletic stride, the carriage of his head, the purposeful way he moved—physically attracted to him, yet guardedly hostile at the same time. It was a curious contradiction, this—being halfway to liking someone, yet resenting both his effect on her and his casual indifference to what she thought of him!

He got into his car, turned it, but at the sound of another car coming down the steep slope where two couldn't meet abreast, he halted and waited until the other—a slightly battered estate car—lurched into view and was pulled inexpertly to a jolting stop by a driver who could only be Donna's uncle, a lean, narrow-shouldered figure, wearing spectacles and a flop-brimmed panama hat. He would have known her as a baby, but they had never met since, and in the snap-shots she had seen of him he had never appeared younger than he did now, nor had he ever been photographed in any but just such an ancient hat.

She stayed where she was, curious to see how the two men would greet each other. They did it with exchanged nods across the width of their cars; whatever the other man said briefly brought her uncle's glance sharply towards the house. Then Elyot Vance drove on, and Wilmot Torrence got out of his car. He was carrying a bundle of books in an ill-secured webbing strap, and as Donna ran down the verandah steps to meet him, the strap slipped and the books cascaded at their feet.

With an exasperated 'Tchah!' he stopped to grope for them before he addressed Donna with a slightly aggrieved, 'Well, so you've arrived. But you were staying over in Antigua tonight—how is it you have got here today?'

She retrieved a book he had missed and handed it to him. 'That was *last* night in Antigua, Uncle. I arrived there by jet from London yesterday, and came down by the island plane today.'

'I'm sure you were to stay two nights in Antigua,' he grumbled. 'That would mean you'd have been here tomorrow, and if you hadn't muddled things so, Bran or I would have met you, of course!'

'But of course I know you would,' Donna soothed.

'Instead you had to accept a lift from that fellow, Vance. Why didn't you telephone from the airport to say you were there, and then wait for Bran or me to come down for you?'

'I did ring you, and spoke to Juno, who said you were both out. And when Mr Vance offered—'

'Putting us under an obligation to him, which must have pleased him no end! I suppose he told you who he was—that he's that—that outsider from Marquise?'

To Donna, 'outsider' was about as outdated an aspersion as 'cad' or 'bounder'. If her father had used it of anyone she would have teased him, 'Oh, Dad, don't be so *square!*' But as she dared not laugh at her uncle in this mood of grievance against both herself and Elyot Vance, she said quietly, 'Yes, we exchanged names and case-histories of a sort, and when I knew he was your neighbour, and that I shouldn't be taking him out of his way, I saw no harm in—' She broke off to add impulsively, 'Anyway,

24

Uncle, does it matter very much? I'm here now, and *so* glad to be! And do you realise I don't remember ever seeing you in the flesh before? Nor Bran? And what do you think of me? Am I much as you expected—or not?'

They looked at each other in silence. Of him she noted how narrow-chested he was, how bony and old—though he could only be about fifty-five—were his hands; how parchment-tanned he was, how his brows beetled over his shortsighted eyes, and how vague was his scrutiny of her.

She doubted whether, put to the test even a minute or two hence, he could come anywhere near to describing her as she would assess herself. Reasonably slim and long-legged; brown hair, centre-parted and shoulder-length; complexion—fresh?, English?, natural?—she wasn't sure. Eyes, grey-green—she would have preferred them green, but except in certain lights, had to settle for grey; one dimple, and a nose which flattery would call retroussé or tip-tilted, but which honesty knew was merely upturned or even snub. There was nothing at all 'rose-bud' about her lips; her mouth was too wide; her father often teasingly warned her against stretching it further with laughter . . .

But in answer to her invitation of 'Well?'

all her uncle said was, 'Well, I've seen your photograph, so I knew what to expect. You've a nice colour and there's a look of your father about you. But all you young girls are pretty much alike these days, with your figures as skinny as laths and your hair as straight as rope. I suppose you've seen Juno, and she knows you're here?'

Donna told him yes, and carried some of the books for him into the house. Glancing at their titles she saw they were botanical treatises and she remembered what she had heard about his hobby—the study of Caribbean flora. Some time she must ask him about it, for if she had ever known the names of the island flowers, she had long forgotten all but the bougainvillea and the poinsettia which everybody knew.

Her room was at the far end of the bungalow, with a little outside stairway of six steps to the lawn below. Juno showed her to it, demonstrated how the window-shutters worked—('But we only close dem against de rain,'), turned down the bed, and to Donna's inquiry about a mosquito net, stated firmly, 'No need. No mosquitoes on Laraye no more,' making it a fact with which there was no dispute.

By the time Donna had unpacked and

26

showered and changed the early dark of the tropics was falling. There had been a golden sunset over the sea, the day wind had dropped and the crickets and the tree-frogs had begun to rival each other's chorus, and hearing them again in reality, she thought, 'I never knew how I missed them until now.'

She returned to the living room to find the table laid for the evening meal and her uncle on the verandah, drinking a rum punch, with ice and passion-fruit juice, and she chose the same for herself. She had expected that by now her cousin Bran might be home, but when she asked about him, his father's tone made such a grievance of their never knowing when to expect him that she was discouraged from discussing Bran any further for the moment.

He had still not arrived when Juno served their dinner of minced beef and sweet potatoes with a coleslaw salad, followed by a gateau which owed more to stodgy sponge than to cream or icing. Her uncle ate as if it were a chore which bored him, and Donna found herself wondering whether his obvious lack of interest in food had ever irked his wife, who had died while Bran was a schoolboy of twelve. But perhaps he had been different then. More—alive.

27

For two people with business interests more or less in common, their talk over the meal was rather laboured. Wilmot asked after his brother and sister-in-law, whether the former had a substitute secretary for Donna, and how the business was doing at the English end. But the answers she gave him led to no expansion of the subject, and her own careful questions to him evoked much the same lack-lustre response.

Poor, was his laconic verdict on the current banana harvesting. As had been the last; as would probably be the next. He couldn't afford the necessary labour force, and once laid off, it got snapped up by the big estates which could 'carry' a few bad crops. A combination of sharp practice and inherited wealth could send the owners of thousand-acre estates, like Marquise, laughing all the way to the bank. It was poor, small plantations like Louvet which had no slack to take up when things went wrong.

Donna winced slightly at 'sharp practice'. Elyot Vance was too sure of himself and hypercritical of other people. But, reluctant to think of him as a cheat, she made no comment, and asked instead about Bran and his particular role on the estate.

'*Bran?*' Wilmot's tone dismissed Bran. 'If

ever I had to depend on *his* application to the job, I'd be out of luck. Growing bananas—or anything else—isn't his scene, he says, whereas the social one is, it seems. He wants to work for and with people of his own kind, he claims. And at the moment, that means getting on the tourist band-wagon, acting as a kind of freelance guide to the island, for one of the hotel owners—a woman—who runs a tour service on the side. On call by telephone at any hour, if you please—a common taxi-driver, no less!' Bran's father finished in distaste.

Donna suppressed a sigh and abandoned the subject of Bran as being unprofitable to any accord with her uncle. What could she say or ask him which wouldn't lead to yet another sour tirade? Ah, perhaps his hobby— But before she could frame a question, Juno came through from the adjoining room, Wilmot's estate office, where she had answered the telephone.

'Mister Brandon,' she announced. 'He ring to say he on late drive with party into mountains. He not come home after. He sleep with Missus le Conte instead—'

'He's doing *what*?' exploded Wilmot with a violence of which Donna would have judged his dourness incapable. But Juno only beamed her innocence of an unforgivable *gaffe*.

'He stay at de hotel, like he done before—often. Missus le Conte find him spare room. Back to breakfast in morning, he say,' she amended calmly.

'That's better,' growled Wilmot. 'All right.' He let her go, then rose from the table. 'Yes, well—it's early yet,' he said awkwardly to Donna, 'but I daresay you're tired after your journey, and I've got some work to do. So if you would like to make an early night of it, you needn't stay up for me.'

Donna was not tired, but though too early as it was for bed, she was not unwilling to escape to her room. She had remembered her little private flight of steps to the outdoors; no one was going to know if she made a small foray into a night that was as warm as an English June day, before she wasted the rest of it—her very first night!—in sleep.

She had not even put on a coat when she tiptoed down the steps and picked her way across the rough grass in the direction of the sea. At the far edge of the grass there was a hedge of russet-leaved crotons; beyond the hedge the land dropped sharply down to the shore, a small crescent of sand, reached by a flight of uneven rock steps, on which the tideless sea lapped and curved, sometimes lazily, sometimes with a surging rush of foam, as if to show that mere wavelets were not all it could muster when it liked. For less sheltered coves than this, the foam warned, it had plenty of menace and rollers in reserve.

Donna went through a gap in the crotons, but did not venture down to the shore. Whenever she had been able to, she loved to swim after dark. But before she swam here she must ask about currents and under-water shelving; for now it was enough to stand and stare—out to sea between the two horns of land which made a bay of the Anse Louvet, up at the velvet of the sky, and at the dark silhouettes of the coconut palms, sturdily rooted in nothing but sand, their trunks aspiring straight to heaven, their fretting topknots of fronds umbrellas for outsized giraffes, no less!

She sighed for utter happiness in the moment. Behind her was an uninspiring house at odds with itself; problems which she had come to Laraye to look at and try to help to iron out if she could; a diplomatic road she would have to tread very warily—all this, with the addition of a neighbour who irked her too easily, yet intrigued her against her will. But probably, with what sounded like a

31

no-man's-land of estrangement between him and her uncle, she would not have to see too much of *him*.

And anyway, she decided on a 'high' of enchantment with the warmth and the lovely night and the promise of tomorrow's sun, nothing was going to spoil the magic of this island for her. Nothing at all!

CHAPTER TWO

Donna woke early to the beat of rain on the roof. But after it had stopped abruptly, as at the turning of a tap, she slept again, and when she had dressed and gone through to the verandah, her cousin was already at breakfast there. A used place showed that her uncle had already eaten and left.

Bran, two years her junior, was tall and loose-limbed, with a mop of fair curly hair and blue eyes, both features in sharp contrast to the deep tan of his skin. At sight of Donna he stood to greet her with a peck of a kiss on her cheek, then held her off and said, 'Surprise, surprise! If we'd known you were coming yesterday we'd have baked a cake— Instead, I gather you stepped off on the wrong foot with Dad by accepting a lift from our friend and neighbour, Vance? How come?'

'Because,' said Donna, 'he was at the airport and you weren't, and he offered, after he'd seen me waiting around for nearly an hour.'

'Yes, well—we seem to have got the dates mixed,' said Bran easily. 'Sorry about that. But let's have a look at you. Last picture I remember of you, you were in a swim suit on a beach—rather puddingy, with a moon-wide grin. But you've slimmed down a lot, haven't you? You're quite a gal, though my word, don't you need a tan! How long are you staying? What do you think of our pad? And how did Elyot Vance strike you, *before* Dad had his say? Anyway, come and eat. Rolls and coffee and fruit juice do you? Or do you want eggs?'

Donna declined eggs, took her place at the table and answered his questions in reverse order. Of Elyot Vance she said, 'He rather put my back up when I overheard him criticising Uncle Wilmot to another man at the airport, and he was pretty high-handed about refusing to take no to his offer of a lift. Rather sure of himself isn't he? Enjoys his success?'

'And *how*—and with reason, I daresay,' Bran agreed. 'More than a bit of the Midas golden touch to Elyot V. Seems he can't go wrong with Marquise, with his work force, with women—Sure you didn't fall flat yourself for the oomph he has for all the girls?'

'Far from it,' Donna denied loftily. 'He's got "poisonality", I'll give him that. But as I told you, he rubbed me up from the start, and I only let him drive me here because he said it was all on his way, and juggernauted me into accepting.' She went on to answer Bran's other questions. 'I've fallen in love with this place—the situation and the *view*, and swimming from your own private bit of beach—superb! As to staying, well, perhaps for as long as Uncle and you will have me. Or until—' She stopped, not quite sure how to word the truth which ought to come next.

'Until—' Bran supplied for her—'you've learned all you came to find out about Louvet and have enough grisly facts to report back? All right, all right,' he soothed as Donna flushed and looked away. 'Not so difficult to read between the lines of Uncle George's letters that he and the Company are worried pink, and that you're not his "and Son" for nothing, eh? Though why didn't he come himself, one is entitled to ask? Why send you on this cloak-and-dagger effort to see what we're up to over here?'

Donna said a little desperately, 'Look, I wanted to come. It *is* a holiday for me. But since, as you must know very well, Louvet hasn't been pulling its weight for ages, Father didn't see any harm in briefing me to see if I could find out why. For one thing, whether Uncle Wilmot has cause for such a chip on his shoulder as he has, and for another, why *you* seem to have opted out.'

Bran's hands, clasped behind his head, pushed his head forward in a leisurely nod. 'Information straight from the grass roots of your wide experience of us and our land and our conditions, no doubt?' he mocked. 'Well maybe I can save you the trouble of a probe in depth. Dad's grouse is that his heart isn't in the banana industry and never was. And I'm getting out because there's no future in it on land that's in the state that Louvet is and has been for the last three years or so. Waste of energy to flog a dead horse. But you won't have seen Louvet yet, will you?'

'No,' said Donna. 'But I want to. Could you take me over it?'

'Sorry, no, not today. I've other fish to fry presently. You'll have to wait until Dad

shows up. He may be over there now. It lies
half a mile or so on, up the hill and on the far
side of the road—' Bran jerked a thumb in
that direction. 'But as he's taken the car, it's
more likely he's ditched you to go off south
into the rain forest on a botanising trip.
Anyway, if you can walk, you could take
yourself exploring alone.'

'I might just do that.' Donna added
curiously, 'What *is* it really about Louvet—
apart from your and Uncle's lack of interest?
Why has it gone to seed when, according to
Elyot Vance, the actual land is no worse than
that of Marquise, which he says it joins?'

Bran's eyebrows lifted. 'There's loyalty for
you! You resented having to be obliged to the
man when he offered you a lift, but that
didn't stop you from discussing Dad and the
failure of Louvet on the way!'

'I did nothing of the sort!' Donna
disclaimed hotly. 'I've already told you I
overheard him talking to his friend, which
was when he said that about Louvet; not to
me.' Feeling the exchange was on the edge of
acrimony, she changed the subject. 'Tell me a
bit about yourself,' she invited. 'How did you
get here this morning from this hotel where
you spent the night, wherever it is?'

'The Allamanda, Margot le Conte's place

at Violon Point. I came up by mini-moke—there.'

Donna shaded her eyes, following the direction of his finger pointing outside. 'On that? In it?' she queried of the small square truck with foot-high wooden sides behind a driver's seat and a snub-nosed bonnet. 'Calls itself a motorised vehicle, does it? You could have fooled me. I've seen hand-drawn dust-carts that could give it points for elegance. Does it *go?*'

'Like a bomb,' Bran assured her. 'Eats out of your hand and never turns a hair at the steepest of hairpins—pun, ha, ha. You'll see a lot of them around; they're handy for using on the plantation roads. Anyway, Margot le Conte is too keen a business woman to allow her hire-cars out on private journeys, so I have to have something for transport.'

'I see.' Donna suddenly laughed. 'Guess how Juno announced that you weren't going to be home last night?' When she repeated the message as Juno had delivered it, Bran's own laugh was a shout.

'That—of the cubbyhole under the tiles which Margot almost begrudges me when I've been out on a night tour until the small hours?' he scoffed. 'I must take Juno aside and mention that opportunity would be a fine

37

thing—that the great Margot le Conte isn't for seducing by a mere minion like me.'

'She's your boss? She owns this hotel, the Allamanda?'

'Uh-huh. She inherited it from her father when she was only eighteen; sacked its manager three years later, moved into his apartment "over the shop", and has run it on her own ever since. In five or six years she's made it one of *the* places of the island, and isn't content with that. I came into the picture when she decided that her tourist clients would prefer guides who weren't of the taximan type—chaps they could invite to lunch with them when they were out on day trips, without embarrassment on either side. So into the tours business goes Margot, all sails set. I qualified for the type she was looking for. I know every inch of the island from A to Z. I wanted out from Louvet; the job suits me, and so there you are.'

Donna was doing mental sums. 'Margot le Conte is still quite young, then? And is she French?'

'Only by extraction. She's from Antigua, born of European and Antiguan parents. English is her language, of course, just as it's ours.'

'And is it this success of hers that makes

38

her "the great Margot"?

'That, and her ambition, spelt with a capital A. In fact, two of a kind, you might say—she and Elyot Vance. Both of them convinced that there's room at the top for them, if for nobody else. And neither of them wholly averse to making the climb together, according to coconut radio.'

Donna tilted her head. 'Coconut radio?' she queried.

'Grapevine to you, my love. Dame Rumour.'

'Oh—Yes, I remember. You mean they would combine business forces—or what?'

'Or what. Marital forces joined first, one imagines. Business ones to follow. Anyway, watch this space, all agog like the rest of us.' Bran stretched and stood up. 'Well, I'm off. A cruise ship came in yesterday, and I've got a date with a couple from Milwaukee. Care for a lift into town? I could drop you off half a mile this side of the Allamanda.'

'No, thanks,' said Donna. 'I think I'll swim and then laze. Is it safe?'

'Perfectly.' On his way down the steps Bran paused and turned. How did Dad know that Vance brought you up yesterday?' he asked.

'Their cars met at the foot of the lane, just

as Mr Vance was leaving.'

'And did sparks fly?'

'No. How could they? Mr Vance had done me a kindness.'

'Which would irritate Dad rather than please him. I can hear him—"Under an obligation to the fellow." Are you sure he didn't say as much later anyway?'

Donna smiled wryly. 'In fact he did—word for word.'

'How did I guess?' Bran chuckled, and went on his way.

★   ★   ★

Donna had swum and floated and played in water which caressed like silk. It was still only mid-morning and now she lay prone on dry sand, letting it run through her fingers until she drowsed and presently slept.

She woke with a start and sat up. She hadn't meant to sunbathe for long on her first day and her back was beginning to tingle. She might swim again or—at a small sound behind her she turned to look back at the beach steps. Halfway down, on one of them, sat Elyot Vance, forearms resting on his thighs, some object between his hands.

'Oh,' she said. 'I didn't know—I fell

asleep.' Odd she thought, this guilt at being caught and watched while sleeping. And equally odd, the vulnerable inferiority of the scantily clad in face of the fully dressed. Wishing she had brought a towel as a cover-all, she stood up and was making a business of brushing sand from her body and legs as Elyot Vance joined her.

'Enter slave, bearing gift,' he announced, proffering what he held in his hand.

It was an aerosol can. She took it from him. 'What? Why?' she queried.

'For your private mosquitoes, which probably won't trouble you again, once having sampled your blood and found it tastes no better than ours, about which they're blasé by now. I found I had this unused can at home, so you're welcome to it. You spray it around you as a warning.'

'Thank you, though in fact they haven't bitten me again, even last night, when I expected I'd be sleeping under a net. But my uncle's housekeeper scorned the idea, and I certainly didn't need one.'

'You're making your own entertainment today?'

'Yes. My uncle and cousin are both out.'

'Over on Louvet?'

'No. That is, Uncle Wilmot may be. But

41

Brandon has gone to take an American couple on a tour.' As Donna was wondering whether she ought to offer the hospitality of coffee or a drink in return for the insect-repellant, its donor said, 'Yes, well, it's pay day on Marquise, and I'm taking my manager down to the bank for the cash. I must go. Do you mean to swim again, or are you coming up?'

She told him she must go to the house for some sunburn lotion and going ahead of him up the steps, aware of his critical view of her fiery back and shoulders, she wished again for the protection of a towel or a wrap. Almost any of the boys she knew would have made some such derogatory remark as 'Who's a boiled lobster then?' and have offered to apply the lotion for her. But this man's silent scrutiny merely made her self-conscious, she didn't know why.

He hadn't brought his car down the lane, and when he had left she went in search of Juno, who chided her for courting the sunburn, but was prepared to dab calomine to it with a willing and generous hand.

'You jes like all strangers, but you learn in time, Missus Donna—old man sun, he an enemy till he cooked you brown like me,' she said, and then, 'Mister Vance, he a good man. Mister Wilmot not think so, but he

42

good, very good. Pay his men well, build houses for dem, send dem to hospital when dey sick, every time he see me he say "Hey, Juno" and sometimes take me to Marquise, see my cousin Maria and her man. Dey cook and man for Mister Vance, like me, cook for Mister Wilmot,' she added in explanation.

This was a more generous assessment of their neighbour than Donna had been given to date. Average it out with her uncle's 'outsider', Bran's 'Midas' eaten up by ambition, and her own guarded reaction to his brusquerie, and what did you get? she wondered. Public Benefactor Number One, a monster of hard-bitten greed, the beau ideal of women (Bran again!), or the roughshod-cum-cavalier who could antagonise or disarm almost, as it were, in one breath?

But though she would have liked to demand that the real Elyot Vance should stand up, she was reluctant to discuss him with Juno, so with a non-committal murmur that he had certainly shown kindness to her, she switched the subject to Juno herself, to learn that she was a 'widow woman', that she had no children, and that she had worked for Wilmot Torrence for 'dunna many' years.

Dressed again in slacks and shirt and a coolie hat tied under her chin, Donna found a couple of vases in a cupboard, filled the low one with a spread of hibiscus blossoms, the taller one with sprays of magenta ixora and oleander, and placed them in the living-room where she thought they brightened it considerably. Juno, however, serving a cold lunch of chicken and saffron rice soon after midday, disapproved.

'Dem hibiscus only good for shoeshine boys, polish shoes. No use in house; dead by sunset every night,' she averred in face of Donna's claim that meanwhile they were lovely, and that she wouldn't mind renewing the arrangement every day.

In the afternoon Juno disappeared into her own quarters and Donna decided to follow Bran's directions to the plantation. At the top of the hill, to the left of the road, a whole spacious valley was spread, lush with the dark green of row upon row of banana bullheads—Marquise and Louvet, side by side, the only boundary between them, Donna supposed, being the road which branched off the main one on which she stood, and became a track leading away down-valley as far as her eye could trace it. As she walked down the track, her guess that to her right lay Marquise and to her left lay Louvet was confirmed by a large roadside notice-board claiming the land on which it stood to be *The Marquise Estate. Property of Elyot R. Vance. Estate Manager, M. Couseau,* with a telephone number for the estate office. And as she walked on it became too painfully clear which was prosperous Marquise land, which was neglected Louvet.

Scattered about Marquise, men were working, though none were near the road. Louvet by contrast, seemed completely deserted. On Marquise, where wind and the weight of fruit had caused the main trunks of the plants to lean, they were carefully propped. On Louvet many had leaned, untended, beyond disaster point. Fallen bullheads everywhere added to the natural trash of decaying leaves and fibre which Donna's theory knew was left for the elements to turn to humus for the enrichment of the land. On Marquise every heavy swag of fruit approaching maturity was cosseted against wind and friction and toxic sprays, in enwrapping polythene bags. On Louvet the bullheads also carried fruit, but nakedly, the skins so brown-pitted that they must eventually become rejects, Donna thought.

The pity of it! The waste! Aloud she addressed an absent Elyot Vance. 'I see what you mean,' she murmured slowly, then bestrode the wide ditch between the track and the ranks of plants, treading trash and stumbling over hidden hazards as she walked down the length of one or two rows.

Conditions were no better further into the plantation. It was obvious that no one had cared to keep Louvet in full production for the time that Elyot Vance had mentioned—at least two seasons. Another one in this climate of sun and rain and magically swift growth, and it could be a wilderness, she judged. Yet neither her uncle nor Bran cared enough for it to save it. Only Elyot Vance did, and he was denied it!

On her way back to the road she stopped to look more closely at a new season's plant where so far only the one 'flower' it would bear had emerged—the fat, purple, pointed ovoid heavily a-swing at the end of its ropy stem, which wasn't in fact a flower at all, but a collection of bracts, protective sheaths for the embryo fruit.

She lifted a bract to marvel at the group of tiny downturned fingers beneath it; each finger blossom-tipped, each one a banana-to-be. Her imagination hurried the fingers into girth and length and their gradual upturn as they grew, until each group of fingers, emerging daily from its bract, indeed resembled a green open hand attached radially, hand above hand, to the stem which at maturity would be slashed from the parent plant.

Only her reading and her visits to Kew had taught Donna that this was how it was, and naturally she had never seen the cycle through. Nor was she likely to see even part of it here on Louvet, she realised, with no dedicated enthusiast to care that she should, from first ground shoot to harvest. Elyot Vance must know it all, but she couldn't see *him* troubling to act as her mentor, nor indeed herself accepting his patronage. For he would be patronising, she was sure. And caustic—as he had been already—to her ignorance. Besides, to Wilmot Torrence he was clearly the Enemy, and she supposed that that made him her enemy too.

A pity though that he was such a man-shaped man, so—alive. She would have liked to feel turned upon her that concentrated interest he had had for his friend at the airport; now serious, now genuinely amused, instead of the satirical approach he had used to her. She found herself wondering what was his relationship with his equal in success, the legendary Margot le Conte—what it meant to him and in what terms. Bran's assessment had made it sound rather cold-blooded, calculated. But Donna hazarded that Elyot Vance's blood ran coldly only for people who had little but passing interest and curiosity value for him—as she herself had, once he found out who she was. She had never given herself many marks for intuition, but she felt—wanted to feel—that the woman he meant to marry could rouse fire in him, desire, hot blood. Margot le Conte—it was a romantic sounding name... Would the girl, little older than Donna herself, prove as romantic a figure to match?

As she walked on, past a Marquise acreage which was obviously a nursery for young banana plants, the Devil was massing his clouds again. The air grew heavy and the sudden rain began, at first only pitting the dusty track, but quickly turning it to squelch. The Devil's wife must have given him best, for the sky was totally overcast, and Donna was despairing of shelter when, ahead of her, through the curtain of rain, she discerned a building by the roadside on Louvet land.

She began to run. She would be wet through by the time she reached it, but she had to get out of this down-pour. As she neared it she saw it was too solid an edifice to be, as her dim view of it had suggested, a packing and sorting station for fruit. It was a square, two-storeyed house, and suddenly for Donna a childhood memory stirred.

It was the sugar plantation house which Elyot Vance had said was still there, on the border between the two estates. He hadn't said that it was still occupied, and as she reached it she saw how forlorn and dilapidated it was, how cobwebbed its windows, how blistered and peeling its ancient paintwork.

It would be locked, of course, but the overhang of its upper floor balcony would afford some shelter. She ran in under it, shook herself like a spaniel, and tried the front door. It wasn't locked, and gave creakily to her push on it.

The inside door stood open to rooms which were thick with dust and rubbish, and they smelled musty. A back door gave on to a small walled courtyard. A staircase, some of its treads broken, led to the upper floor. Donna remembered none of it as it was now. She thought there had been a garden and a stone sundial, and that the balcony had been at the back, instead of at the front, facing out over what was now Marquise land. And then—it was built of wood throughout—it

49

had been gaily painted in gypsy reds and greens. It had been as novel to her as if fashioned from gingerbread.

Although the rain had stopped and she meant to make her way back, hotfoot, to the bungalow, she went upstairs for a cursory look round. She crossed a room to the floor-to-ceiling window and found she hadn't to slip its catch to open it. She stepped out on to the balcony, took a step or two towards the outer balustrade, and didn't realise what was happening underfoot until it had.

With a tearing, splitting sound the flooring had given way beneath her weight. Too late to step back on to what may, or may not, have been sound boards, she went down into the V-gap of the broken ones. The V opened to the depth of her own height, and for a sickening moment she thought it would let her fall straight through. But at its point it held by what felt like mere splinters, leaving her in the ludicrous plight—if it had not been so frightening—of being upright with her back against one arm of the V, facing the jaggedness of the other, her feet down to the broken wood at its point.

She could get out. She *must* get out! But her cautious reach forward to the jagged arm only broke away more wood, and her attempt to turn back, in order to claw at the flooring behind her, caused the weakness at the point of the V to splinter further. If she did manage to turn, and it gave completely, she would be left hanging by her hands until she fell... She stayed where she was, not moving.

She felt sick with self-blame. She should have realised the state the woodwork would be in, unpainted and unpreserved against weather for years, it seemed. And how was she to be rescued? And when? Men were still working in the Marquise plantations, but they were too far off to hear her shout. Perhaps when they knocked off work some of them would come along the road, and they would see her if she signalled with—yes, her coolie hat would make a big flapping. Gingerly, hardly daring to risk the movement, she untied its strings, held it by one of them and waited.

Her shirt was sticking painfully to her sunburned back, and her slacks were clammy about her legs. Would those men out there work until sundown? If so, that was hours ahead! And supposing even then, none of them used the road?

But she hadn't to wait hours. At first, from the direction from which she had come, there was the sound of a motor vehicle, then the

51

familiar sturdy shape of a jeep. Careful not to move otherwise, she waved the hat frantically, and the jeep stopped.

The driver was Elyot Vance. After he had jumped down he stood for a moment, staring. Then at a big stride he came over to the house. Donna heard him begin aloud, 'What the—?' Then he went in under the balcony and she heard him run up the stairs and approach the open window.

Over her shoulder she called back, 'Don't step out. The floor is rotten!' To which his reply was a terse 'Obviously,' as he knelt to crawl forward, feeling his way. The floor held, as it had done for her to that point, and when he reached her he ordered, 'Turn round and face me.'

'I—I can't. I've tried. If I move, I shall fall through.'

'You must turn, and help yourself by holding on to the edge while I take the rest of your weight to haul you up. Now!'

She turned. The frail wood at the point of the V broke at the thrust of her scrabbling feet, and the jagged edge of the flooring crumbled again before she gained a firm hold on it. But the strong hands under her armpits upheld her as their owner, still kneeling, edged slowly backward, inch by inch, drawing her heavily with him until she too was able to kneel on firm wood, facing him.

While he had pulled she had looked at him and seen in his taut jaw and clenched teeth and glittering eyes something of the fire which his cool satirical outward bearing masked. But it was no smoulder of passion, nor even of physical effort. His tone left her in no doubt that it was a blaze of anger which drove him to his intensely breathed, 'May the gods give me patience! That anyone could be such a fool—' He broke off, as if words failed him.

Still kneeling, Donna looked down at her clasped hands, trembling from shock and mortification. 'Meaning me,' she murmured, not making it a question.

'By the fool? Who else? If you'd gone right through and down, you might have been killed, or broken some limbs at least!' he retorted.

'I—I might have fallen on my feet, like a cat.' It was a poor attempt at lightness which he scorned.

'Cats have unique fall mechanisms,' he snapped. He stood and took both her hands to draw her to her feet. Without releasing her he went on, 'A wooden house—*wooden*, in this climate!—standing derelict for years, and

you choose to investigate, clamber about it—
Why, the very state of the stairs could have
told you what to expect of an open balcony,
fully exposed to the weather! For pity's sake,
come in off it while some of it's still
underfoot. What were you doing down here
anyway—alone?'

She followed him into the dusty room
through the window and he slipped its catch
shut. She explained, 'I was exploring Louvet,
and when it began to rain heavens hard, I saw
this place and I ran for it. As soon as I got
near, I knew what it was, even though it
looked different—and smaller. But no one
except you had mentioned it to me, and *you*
hadn't said how long it had been derelict and
rotting. So how was I to know it was
dangerous?'

'"Nobody told me." Famous last words,'
he mocked. 'I'd have expected you to be
canny to the sight of those stairs, not to
mention the stink of dry rot in your nose.
However—what's the damage? Are you
hurt?'

'Only bruised, I think. And this—' She
turned the outer side of one wrist to him to
show a long angry graze.

'H'm. You'll need to watch that, keep it
clean and covered. And you're still wet

through.' His hands had reached to feel her shoulders, and he allowed his touch to travel down her body to her hips. His glance ran down the line of her slacks to her knee, where a T-tear gaped, then lifted to her rat-tailed hair in an assessment of her woebegone condition which was as clinical and dispassionate as a doctor's. For a moment she wondered wildly whether she would have rated more sympathy from him if she had indulged in a fit of the vapours, whatever they were. But she decided not. The man was a cold fish who enjoyed putting people in the wrong and then blamed them as fools for being there. Well, anyway, as fools whom he was forced to rescue from their own folly. So where *was* his alleged attraction for women, eh, Bran?—an attraction which she had experienced initially herself, but wouldn't again while, bored, he looked at her and through her without really seeing her at all. And now, she supposed, he would dutifully round off his second bout of knight-errantry in two days by insisting on seeing her home!

He didn't trouble to insist. He took it for granted that he would. When they went out to the jeep he lifted her bodily by the waist and dumped her on to the bench seat beside him, turned the vehicle and drove back up the track. Presently he remarked, 'So your uncle sent you alone to look at Louvet? What do you think of it?'

'He didn't send me. He'd gone out before I was up this morning.' Donna hesitated between loyalty and candour. And as she guessed loyalty would only make for argument, she chose candour. 'It—it's pathetic, isn't it?' she said.

'It's more than that. It's near-criminal,' he said grimly. But that was all. Donna was silent too, knowing he was right.

At the top of the lane to the bungalow she told him he could drop her there, and began to thank him. But he said, 'No. If your uncle has returned, I'd like a word with him. If not, perhaps you'll tell him I shall look in again?'

'You aren't going to make trouble, I hope?' she ventured, as the car standing on the crab-grass was evidence that Wilmot was at home.

'Just as much trouble as the situation calls for.' He braked, alighted, helped her down and made for the verandah. 'Go and get out of those damp things,' he added. But she stayed when she saw that Wilmot was sitting on the verandah, a glass of punch beside him on the table where he was extracting leaves and sprays of foliage from small plastic bags. He stood as they approached. 'Ah, Vance,' he said coldly, and sat again. 'And Donna—where have you been?'

It was Elyot Vance who answered for her. 'She's been exploring Louvet.' he said.

Wilmot's brows went up. 'With you?'

'No. She walked over on her own. Did you know she intended to?'

'Of course not. We haven't met since last night.'

'Then I suppose I can't blame you for not warning her about the state of the Dial House, but the fact remains that she went into it to shelter from the rain, and might well have been killed or badly injured when the balcony caved in as she walked out on it. Fortunately it held long enough until I happened by and was able to help her free. But that was her good luck and yours.' Elyot suddenly exploded. 'For Pete's sake, man, just how long do you mean to leave the place standing to rot away? Are you hoping that one day it will crumble to shavings before your very eyes, saving you the trouble of doing anything about it, or what?'

Wilmot blinked at this attack and looked at Donna. 'You shouldn't have—You should have realised—'

'Of course she should. But she didn't.' The words rapped out. 'And no credit to you if

57

she had. That menace—bang-on to our boundary road; no trespass board nor danger sign; doors and windows unbarred; open to the idle curiosity of any passerby, and what about the risk to children? What about that?'

'There should be no children about there. They have no right on my land.'

'No? Well, they have on mine—with their mothers, my women workers who can't leave them at home. Try telling an adventurous toddler not to wander as we do constantly— still, sooner or later one of them or a bunch are going to make it over to the Dial—and then where might you find yourself in the matter of culpable negligence—tell me that?'

'The house is on my land. No one has the right to trespass into it.' Wilmot maintained doggedly.

'When it doesn't boast so much as a fence or a gate to keep them out?' His opponent's gesture was contemptuous. 'Try making that a plea in a compensation court and see where it gets you!' He paused, then added in a less aggressive tone, 'Look, man, *why* haven't you done anything to put the place together or to raze it, until now?'

'Because I have neither the money nor—'

At that Donna was moved to put in, 'Oh, Uncle, I'm sure the Company could bear the expense, if you would—'

Wilmot ignored her. 'Nor,' he repeated, 'the available labour, as you, Vance, should well know, since you absorb it all at wages which I can't pay. What's more, may I ask whether you've jumped to conclusions on the condition of the Dial only from today's mishap to my niece?'

If Elyot saw the intended trap, he discounted it. 'Oh no,' he admitted. 'I've inspected it thoroughly before now. I assure you, no jump.'

Wilmot pounced. 'Then you've trespassed yourself, but haven't seen fit to approach me about it until now?'

'That's right.' The agreement was bland, almost good-tempered. 'I've trespassed, but the place is your property, it's on your land, and protest was pointless until an accident happened. Now it has.'

'And now—?' Wilmot invited.

'And so, protest, of course.'

'Which you've made—'

'—And an offer to meet you. If, as your niece suggests, Torrence and Son will carry the cost, I'll personally see that you get the men and the tools. How's that?'

'To destroy the place?'

A shrug. 'That's for you to decide.

59

Though'—Elyot Vance glanced at Donna—'I imagine that for old times' sake, your niece would rather it were restored. She remembers it from her childhood, she says.'

'And if I refuse to be "met" in the way you suggest?' Wilmot demanded.

'Then I'm afraid it's ultimatum that you do something yourself, lest the Growers' Association should see fit—'

Wilmot stood again, drawing himself to his full lanky height. 'Are you *threatening* me with action by the Growers' Association, young man?' he questioned.

'Far from it.' The other's smile was disarming. 'I'm merely a humble member of the Association, and you're another, neither of us with a say in the high-ups' decisions on sanctions. But if you won't accept help from your own Company or from me, alternatively why not persuade your son that he could do worse by you than to take off his shirt and collect a few of his cronies to take on the job in their ample spare time?'

Wilmot was almost gibbering. 'Thank you,' he said. 'When I find myself in need of advice from you, I'll ask for it. Until then—'

Elyot's nod appeared to accept the sweet reason of that. 'Any time,' he said, and to Donna, 'Get in there and change, and have

Juno bandage that wrist'—an order which she did not obey. As he turned from them both, he added to Wilmot, 'Meanwhile, my offer remains open—indefinitely,' and went down the verandah steps.

'You may consider it closed- -definitely,' Wilmot called after him, and sat down, drumming angry fingers on the table edge and muttering.

Donna ventured, 'Uncle, I don't think you should have antagonised him so. That house *is* dangerous as it stands, and his offer to provide the men to work on it was generous, you can't deny.'

Wilmot erupted. 'Trespass! Nosing around! Telling me my own business! Hinting "or else". Trying the power game— with me!' He eyed Donna with suspicion. 'That's twice in two days that the fellow has wormed his way in here; foisted himself on you first, and then on me. You haven't, I hope, encouraged him, by any chance?'

If Donna hadn't been so outraged by the accusation, she could have laughed. 'It so happens,' she reminded Wilmot, 'that twice in two days he's been there when I needed someone—this afternoon, rather badly. He didn't have to be encouraged to do for me what any decent man would in the same circumstances, I hope. Both times he did it, and I'm grateful.'

'Yes, well,' her uncle yielded slightly, 'I thought you might have been flattered. He has an easy way with women, one understands—'

'So Bran hinted of him as well,' Donna cut in. 'But I'm not as impressionable as all that, and I do rather object to being lumped together with "Women" who may have fallen for his alleged charm.'

'Yes, well,' Wilmot conceded again, 'I suppose I can trust you to take care of yourself and keep men like him at arm's length. I certainly hope so, for in Bran's set in and around the Allamanda and the beach clubs, you can hardly help meeting him. Just so long as you don't expect me to welcome him here!' he concluded sourly.

At that Donna felt she had had enough as the present pawn in this bitter long-drawn game between her uncle and his neighbour.

'After this afternoon, do you suppose he'd be over-eager to come?' she asked and, getting no answer, went through to her room, feeling defeated and depressed and wondering whose side she was supposed to be on.

When she had discarded her soiled shirt

and torn slacks, changed into a flowered shift dress and managed to bandage her wrist herself, she felt a little better.

But what a plunge from her blissful euphoria of last night! Where had the magic gone? The natural loveliness which had inspired her mood then hadn't changed. The sea and the sky, the warmth and the peace were still all there; only today's personal clashes were the despoilers. She hated quarrels, and she hated this old one because, through no fault of her own, it tore her two ways.

Odd, that yesterday she had been unmoved by, had even welcomed the thought of having to see little or nothing more of Elyot Vance, and yet today she had resented Wilmot's edict against him. Whose side *was* she on, for goodness' sake? Two encounters with the man, both of them weighted against her, yet if he did keep his distance in future, she was actually going to miss a challenge which could be likened to the abrasive rub of sandpaper on the skin—painful, but stimulating at the same time.

So just how illogical, in the space of twenty-four hours, was it possible to get?

CHAPTER THREE

It seemed that Wilmot saw nothing questionable in his having allowed Donna to make her own first foray to the plantation, and whereas in London and on the journey over she had visualised his being ready and willing to give the information which her father would want to hear, it was she who had to ask the questions and then to edit the lacklustre answers so as not to paint too dismal a picture of conditions on Louvet in her first letters home.

Of the Dial House incident she said nothing. Her father probably did not realise it still existed, and her own mishap would only worry him. She mentioned having met Elyot Vance, and for Laraye itself she was full of enthusiasm. There was time enough, she felt, to tell more when she knew more of the complicated issues at stake.

She swam and sunbathed every day; made one tentative suggestion that she might help in the office with paper work for the estate— an offer which Wilmot refused; went down to the town by jitney, the local bus, to shop for Juno in the markets, and at unpredictable intervals had fleeting encounters with Bran, who usually seemed to be on his way to or from somewhere else.

She walked often in the plantation where a few men worked, though not regularly and never, during Donna's first two or three weeks, on the weekly crop-consignment day, when they and their womenfolk defected, freelance, to Marquise and other estates to earn more than Wilmot paid them, by helping to harvest and grade and pack and despatch that week's crop for refrigerated shipment to England by the fleet of white cargo-ships which ran shuttlewise back and forth across the Atlantic.

During those weeks Louvet cropped nothing for consignment. That was how it was, Wilmot grumbled. If you harvested too soon the crop would be rejected as unready; if you left it too late you risked over-ripeness or theft. According to Wilmot the small grower just couldn't win; the titans like Marquise couldn't lose.

Marquise could corner the market in labour. Marquise could afford to spray by air against disease and pests. Marquise could build modern sheds for grading and packing. Marquise could coddle its growing crops in polythene. Marquise could keep five hundred acres in continual cultivation... so what could the small man do against competition like that? None of which seemed to Donna to add up to one good reason for Wilmot's retention of Louvet in face of Elyot Vance's willingness to relieve him of it. But that was an argument which at this stage of her ignorance she dared not put forward.

It was on the Saturday of her third week that Bran suggested taking her to dine at the Allamanda and to be 'introduced around'. Margot le Conte was giving a cocktail party for the hotel guests and had suggested that he should take Donna along.

'Do we have to go down in the mini-moke?' she asked, fearful for her hair-do and an evening dress in that primitive vehicle.

'No. Dad will let us have the car,' Bran promised. 'And doll up a bit, won't you? Those American women tourists do rather tend to lay on all they've got by way of window-dressing in the evening. You don't want to look country cousin by contrast.'

Meaning *you* don't want me to look country cousin to your friends, thought Donna as she 'dolled up' to the best of her ability in one of the lightweight evening dresses she had brought with her. It was of mist-grey chiffon over a satin underslip, the skirt falling from an Empire-style high bodice of silver lurex. She wore silver slippers, carried a silver tapestry bag and piled her hair high under a silver net snood.

Bran approved. Juno did not. 'Grey colour—dat for old women. Red, yellow, nice pink for young girl like you, Missus Donna. Gay shawl,' she advised. Wilmot grudgingly allowed that he supposed she looked 'all right'. Donna herself had liked what her mirror had shown her, and went out to meet her evening in a lighthearted party mood.

Violon Point was one 'horn' of the almost landlocked Violon Bay, one of the show-places of the island. The Allamanda Hotel, a long split-level building behind a many-arched colonnade of latticed stonework, faced the palm-fringed shore on a lengthy frontage. Every balcony on every floor was hung with trails of bougainvillea and morning glory, and the wide lawns behind the building were ablaze with the golden bells of allamanda blossom which gave the place its name. Though it was not long after dusk when Bran and Donna arrived, flood-lamps were already lighting and silhouetting the tops of the palms against the sky, and beyond the range of the lights, the deep jungle green of the surrounding heights had turned to impenetrable black.

'It's quite a place,' murmured Donna in admiration.

'And quite a gal in possession,' returned Bran. 'Come and meet her. She's dying to meet you.'

'Dying? She can't be!'

'She says so.'

And that, Donna was to realise before the evening was out, was the very essence of the just-that-bit-larger-than-life character which was Margot le Conte.

Her greeting for Donna the stranger was a kiss on each cheek and a murmured, 'Darling! Bran didn't say how pretty you are'—a compliment which might have pleased Donna more if she hadn't noticed that almost every other one of Margot's guests, including the men, was made welcome with a similar double kiss and word of flattery, implying a warmth which, Donna decided, Margot couldn't possibly feel for them all.

She spoke by gesture almost as readily as in the deep contralto of her voice. Everything she said or did was touched with extravagance, over-emphasis. With her, a beckoning finger became an imperious movement of her whole hand in her direction. She used it to call servants and guests alike, who, when she had done with them, were dismissed with an equally exaggerated backward wave. She smiled often, showing excellent teeth behind parted full lips. She carried her head on a long slender neck; her features were fine-drawn, her small nose a perfect aquiline; her skin—face, throat, bare arms and shoulders—had the velvet glow of a ripe peach; the heavier side of her black hair hung provocatively forward; her eyes were so dark as to be nearly black. In a bronze sheath of a dress which revealed every curve of her slim body she was as lissom as a yearling cat, as physically delicate as her manner was poised and assured. If she were indeed a tycoon she was a devastatingly glamorous one. In contrast with her, every other female in the room, including herself, had the makings of a country cousin, thought Donna, watching her.

She detached Donna from Bran almost at once, carrying her off in a babble of introductions to other people. It soon became apparent that it was as much a party for Margot le Conte's own friends as it was for her hotel clients, and after a time and some circulation the two sets tended to separate.

Presently again some people drifted away to the dining-room, others of the locals thanked their hostess and went home, leaving behind a few lingerers from the hotel set and a nucleus of Margot's own friends who had gathered to sit at a long oval table, seemingly prepared to make an evening of it for drinks and talk. Elyot Vance wasn't among them; he hadn't appeared at the party at all, surprising Donna who, after Wilmot's drear prophecy that she would have to meet him in the Allamanda set, had fully expected him to be there.

Meanwhile Donna's healthy young appetite was signalling its willingness to dine, and she looked about for Bran. But he was part of the hard core of the group at the table, and when she failed to catch his eye, she despaired of dinner in the immediate future. Instead she wandered off alone towards the soft murmur of the sea, lapping just below one of the arches of the ground-floor colonnade. She went to lean upon the waist-high stone balustrade where the flowers from the arch on the floor above trailed low enough to form a kind of scented pelmet for this one.

Behind her, people passed and repassed on their way to or from the car-park, but she was left alone to enjoy the night sounds and the sea sounds and the teasing of a tiny breeze until someone halted behind her and waited for her to turn about.

It was Elyot Vance. Without preliminaries he said, 'I told myself, "That's a back view I know," and it was. How is the sunburn?'

Taken by surprise, she laughed awkwardly. 'I've tanned now, and I don't burn,' she said.

'And the mosquitoes?'

'They've left me alone since that first day.'

'And the grazed wrist?'

'That's better too. You make me sound terribly disaster-prone,' she added.

'Well, you weren't exactly among the blest of the gods when we last met, were you?' he countered easily. 'But why are you alone? What about the party?'

'It isn't over. I was waiting for my cousin to take me in to dinner.'

'Still involved, is he? And you're hungry?'

'Tending that way.'

'So let's go and prise him free.'

As soon as they appeared Margot hurried over from where she had been standing by the table, her hand on the shoulder of one of her men guests.

She held her arms wide to Elyot and offered her cheek for him to kiss. 'Elyot,

71

you're late,' she said, and to Donna. 'Clever of you to corral him, darling. Where?'

'I found her,' Elyot answered for Donna. 'Alone, communing with the night, but about ready to start chewing the carpet in need of her dinner.'

Margot commiserated. 'You poor lamb! I'll call "Time, gentlemen," to Bran this very next minute. But you, Elyot, you wretch, why are you so late? I declare, you've been *cinq à sept* with another woman!'

He laughed and pulled a strand of her swinging hair. 'When I spend useful afternoon hours with a woman, that'll be the day,' he said.

'Before now, you've spent an afternoon with me!'

'Talking business.'

'But not *all* the time!' Margot sparkled archly. 'Anyway, come and have a drink and I'll tell Bran he must take Donna in to dinner—or else!'

But when Bran had detached himself from the group of drinkers Elyot declined a drink. 'Maurice Couseau and I had one together at the Yacht Club, and I'm driving,' he said.

'You'll dine, though'

'I'd like to, yes.'

Bran looked at Margot. 'Then make a

foursome of it, why don't we?' he suggested.

Margot hesitated. 'Yes, well—' But Elyot took her masterfully by the elbow.

'I'm hungry too, so you'll eat now and like it,' he ordered.

The whole length of one side of the dining room was open to the warm night. Electric fans whirred from the ceiling, and a steel band beat out dance-rhythms at intervals for people to dance between courses. Margot had a word or two with her head waiter, approved the position of the table he offered, and before she sat down, made a tour of the other tables, chatting briefly with each of the guests.

When she rejoined the others Elyot quipped. 'The conscientious keeper making sure all his valuable charges are fed and happy, eh?' At which she snapped a finger and thumb smartly against his hand.

'All part of the service, man,' she said. 'When I make you co-director of the Allamanda, you'll learn how a little bonhomie pays.'

During the meal that was the keynote of their exchanges—a slightly brittle scoring-off each other, playfully by Elyot, less so by Margot, whose repartee was occasionally touched with malice. They evidently knew each other very well, thought Donna, envying them a little an association which seemed to shut other people out. Yet how close they really were it was difficult to tell.

The four were waiting for their coffee to be brought when Elyot asked Margot to dance. When they walked out on to the floor they were the only couple on it, and soon after they began to dance it was as if by common consent that they were left to a display which was not far short of exhibition quality.

The syncopated beat of the drums slowed and quickened, repeating phrases over and over, now sonorous, now wailing in the accompaniment to the repetitive words of a calypso, all in a perfectly maintained monotonous tempo. And, encouraging and rejecting in turn Elyot's stylised advance and retreat, Margot forsook all decorum in her abandonment to the dance; in turn sensuous, provocative, tempting her partner and repulsing with mimed modesty the implicit invitation of his approach.

Her steps were nothing remarkable, an easy heel-and-toe movement only. All her expression was in her threatrical use of hands and arms, slim body, arched throat and wildly flung black hair. The whole performance became a man-to-woman question and answer, and Donna, fascinated, thought, *To this extent they know each other very well. They've done this together often before.*

The music stopped, their audience clapped them off the floor and several other couples moved on to it. Back at the table, poised and collected again, Margot ordered sharply, 'Bran, do your duty by your pretty cousin—take her to dance,' but Elyot cut in, 'My privilege before a mere cousin,' and held out his hand to Donna.

She went with him, dreading the inevitable contrast with Margot's expertise. But to her surprise and half relief, half chagrin that he didn't expect her to compete, he took her in his arms and steered her smoothly through the same old-fashioned slow foxtrot which the older couples were doing. Tactful of him, of course. But a shade belittling, all the same!

Presently Margot and Elyot danced with other people and Bran asked Donna if she wanted to. But she said no, and then urgently, 'Bran, what does *cinq à sept* mean?

He looked at her sharply. 'Why, "five till seven", of course. You can count to ten in French, surely?'

'Of course I can. But what *does* it mean?'

'In what connection?'

75

'Well, when Elyot Vance arrived late, Margot accused him of having been "*cinq à sept*" with another woman, and he had to laugh it off.'

'Yes, well—' Bran sounded embarrassed— 'it's a French vulgarity for accusing a man of spending the late afternoon, say five o'clock till seven, with his girl-friend before going home to dinner with his wife.'

'Oh,' said Donna blankly.

'What do you mean—oh?' Bran retorted. 'Why the surprise? I told you the kind of terms they're on. And you've seen them together.'

'Yes, but—'

'And Margot's not the girl to be too delicate about claiming her monopolies, especially with another one there to be warned Keep Out.'

'But I was the only one there to hear her,' Donna objected.

'And you're feminine and you came in with Elyot, didn't you?'

'Yes, but she couldn't have thought—'

'That you were any competition? No, probably not,' Bran agreed with cousinly candour, adding sagely, 'But I imagine women at the top like Margot don't care to suspect anyone of trying to climb their private ladder—anyone at all.'

As that dance ended they saw a desk clerk approach Margot, and after speaking to him and excusing herself to her partner, she came back to the table, followed by Elyot. When he waited for her to sit she gestured, 'No,' adding to Bran, 'It's your buddies from Milwaukee. They're flying home tomorrow and they've taken a fancy for a last night-view of the island from the mountains, so they want you to drive them.'

Bran groaned, 'Oh, *no*! It's my night off duty!'

'And he's been drinking,' Elyot put in.

'Only punches, and he's had a meal since. He's all right,' Margot ruled crisply. 'No, Bran, I've sent back a message to say you'll go. Seems you've wormed your way into their affections and they won't have anyone else. Besides, The Customer Is Always Right.'

Bran grumbled, 'You said it, ma'am—I didn't.' But he half rose, then stopped. 'How long for?' he asked.

'As long as they want to be out, of course.'

'I see. Maxim for maxim—he who pays the piper calls the tune, eh?'

'Exactly. It's the name of the game of success,' returned Margot smoothly. 'Go along now. They'll be waiting.'

'But what about Donna? Do I take her home first?'

'No, she can stay here until you come back. You probably won't be more than an hour away at most.' As he left, Margot added to Donna, 'Sorry about this, darling, but it's all business, and you didn't want to go home yet, did you?'

This being one of those questions expecting no for an answer, Donna said it, and Margot went on, 'Besides, I want to talk to you. Can you drive?'

Surprised, Donna said 'Yes.'

'And you've got one of those international licences?'

'Yes. Why?'

'Time on your hands too, I daresay? Not much going for you up there at Louvet, hm?'

'Well—' Donna hesitated, not sure where all this was leading. But as certainly, with Bran so often absent and Wilmot indifferent to her company, she was thrown much more on her own resources and Juno's than she had expected, she admitted she did have time to spare, and again asked, 'Why?'

'Because I've been thinking I could use you. How would you like to work for me? Doing the same as Bran—playing guide to my tourists?'

Donna's first reaction was of astonishment and recoil. 'Oh, I couldn't,' she demurred. 'I don't know the island as Bran does, and your roads are pretty hair-raising, aren't they?'

'If you enjoy driving and can, you'd soon get used to them. Besides, all my cars are automatic, and they eat out of your hand. And my idea was that, whenever Bran has only two passengers or one, you should go along with him for a while and learn the island. He tells me you spent some of your childhood here, so you probably will find you remember parts of it. And if, as he says too, you were hankering to come back, how else can you get to explore it in comfort and in company, tell me that?'

That was an adroit argument on Margot's part. Donna had wondered what prospects she had of travelling much further afield than to Calvigne by jitney or the occasional trip in her uncle's car, and she was tempted. But her memory of Wilmot's disapproval of Bran's defection from Louvet held her back. 'You are right,' she told Margot. 'I've wondered how I could see more of Laraye while I'm here, but I don't think my uncle would care for me to take a job.'

'It wouldn't occupy you every day. You wo d only be on call when I needed you—

say, to take out ladies who would rather be driven by a girl than a man. You might make some very good friends that way,' Margot urged.

'Yes. Well, supposing I went out with Bran as you suggest, and tried handling a car, and spoke to my uncle, perhaps I could help out when you needed someone. I don't think I'd like to promise more than that,' Donna said.

Margot shrugged. 'Fair enough. Go out with Bran, make him let you take the driving sometimes and use your eyes and ears when he does his running commentary on the sights. Particularly, get hold of the names of the flowers and the trees and have the life-cycle of the crops—the bananas and the aubergines and pineapples and coconuts—at your fingertips. People pay to be informed, and informed they will be, or know the reason why.'

'And you may be sure, with Margot in control, that they *pay*,' Elyot put in, in a dry aside to Donna.

'Of course. I'm a businesswoman. But I give value for money by using people like Bran and Donna, instead of taxi-boys, a lot of whom only know the names of things in *patois* and consequently can't even spell them out, since *patois* isn't written,' Margot snapped back.

'And when Donna has acquired all this gen do you propose putting her on formal test?' he asked.

'I'd like to. And you'd like to show off, wouldn't you, darling? Rather fun, don't you think, if I played the dumbest of dumbwits who's never seen a banana or an aubergine except in a supermarket or on a fruit barrow, and thinks orchids are rare hothouse freaks that only rich brides' bouquets can afford?' Margot appealed to Donna, who smiled and agreed, realising she was meant to.

An hour passed; nearly two. There was more dancing—Donna partnered once with Elyot, again in a sober waltz, and with a couple of men to whom she had been introduced before dinner. When Elyot went to the bar with a friend, Margot took Donna to see what she called 'my modest pad'—her private apartment on the top floor, the decor and furnishing of which were exotic in the extreme.

Margot took her leisure in a twenty-five-foot salon, glass-panelled all along the seaward side; sunbathed on a screened verandah, bathed in an emerald green marble sunken bath and slept in a king-size bed under a white satin canopy in an all-white bedroom. Though Donna found the whole effect rather overwhelming she murmured in suitable awe, 'It's terribly *luxe*,' to which Margot replied complacently, 'I planned it that way. I'm a bit of a *luxe* person myself, and I do need the best of everything around me—you know?'

She had sat to comb her hair at the dressing-table mirror when Elyot came up to say that Bran had telephoned and that he had taken the call. 'He's in trouble,' Elyot announced.

'Trouble?' Frowning, Margot swung round on the stool. 'What?'

'Not serious, and not his fault,' Elyot assured her. 'It seems he's had a difference with a jitneyful of revellers, the driver among them, on their merry way home from a Saturday night hoedown. The jitney had stopped—to put down some passengers, Bran supposed—just ahead of his car. But instead of going on when it did start up, it charged backward on to his bonnet and tried to climb it.'

'Tch, the fools! Is our car damaged?' Margot demanded.

'Apparently not much, but when they'd prised them apart, the whole busload of passengers fell upon Bran, accusing him of running them down. They wouldn't listen to reason, so the upshot is that he and his own passengers have had to go to the police station in Marc d'Assau to give evidence. That's a one-horse place in the mountains,' Elyot explained to Donna. 'Everything is being taken down in longhand with a well-licked pencil, and Bran's bother is that he doesn't know when he can get free to take you home.'

Margot said again, 'Tch! That car was new last month. Are the other two, the Milwaukee couple, very annoyed?'

'Why should they be? They've suffered no damage, they wanted a night out and they're only delayed. They'll probably dine out on the story as a bit of Caribbean local colour for weeks to come. Meanwhile, what about Donna?' Elyot asked.

'Oh. Yes. We'll send her home by taxi, of course.'

'No. I'll take her myself.'

'Please don't bother. I can easily—'

'But, Elyot, you don't want to go yet?'

Donna and Margot had spoken together, and he answered Donna, 'It's all on my way,' and Margot, 'Yes, I'll go now, while my alcohol intake is minimal,' ignoring her annoyed, 'Tiresome of you!' which embarrassed Donna, but which he ignored.

In the foyer they said their goodnights to Margot, and as they got into Elyot's car, Donna remarked, 'This is becoming a bit of a cliché, isn't it?'

'A cliché?'

'Stereotyped, repetitive—your having to volunteer transport for me so often, I mean.'

'And should I reply gallantly that for me it's a pleasure which bears repeating, or risk offending you with a blunt reference to Hobson's choice? Perhaps I'd better play safe with a neutral "You're welcome," which can say as little or as much as you care to let it. Anyway, what are you feeling about Margot's proposal?' Elyot asked after a pause.

'I think I'd like to try it occasionally, but it depends on what Bran will say to toting me around while I learn the ropes, whether I can master the driving, and my uncle's reaction to the idea,' Donna said.

'Well, you should find the driving nothing of a problem once you've had a bit of practice; your cousin will like anything that Margot orders of him—she's that kind of woman, and with your uncle you must use all the diplomacy you know.'

'Yes, though I shouldn't care to take it on if he doesn't want me to.' She changed the subject. 'Tell me, on these guided tours, *may* one take people quite freely on to the plantations? For instance, since there wouldn't be much profit in showing them Louvet, could I take them on to yours, Marquise?'

'Be my guest. It's all publicity for the trade.'

'Thank you.' There was silence then until Elyot suggested, 'I suppose tonight was your first experience of dancing to a genuine, dyed-in-the-wool steel band on its own home ground?'

'You mean out here, where playing on steel originated? Yes.'

'Originated of necessity, when the boys couldn't afford any instruments but cut-down dustbins. Do you like the rhythm?'

'It grows on you.'

'It does more than that for some people. It gets deep into their blood. Into Margot le Conte's for one. You may have realised that she hasn't many inhibitions to start with, but to a Caribbean beat of any quality, she abandons the lot and dances, stripped of every rag of reserve, as it were. As *you* couldn't, I take it, to anything like the same degree?'

Donna agreed, 'No. It must be quite an experience, dancing with her?'

'It is. Unique.'

'Which was probably why—' she couldn't help asking to make sure—'you chose to do only sedate fox-trots with me, knowing I couldn't compete?'

He appeared to ponder the question. Then—'You could say that. You're English. Margot is not. One couldn't look for the same degree of verve. On the other hand—'

Donna waited. At last she prompted, 'On the other hand—what?'

'Well, I'd also admit that a man does like to vary his style—refreshing, you know, to get away from the jungle tactics that the drums demand, to the Blue Danube approach of having a girl in your arms, close enough to know she's really there, not one to five yards away and retreating.'

'I see,' said Donna gravely.

He laughed. 'You don't. You'd have liked to show off what you could do. But let it ride for now, and perhaps I'll let you—next time.'

When they reached the top of the lane, as she had done once before, she asked him to drop her there. But he refused.

'When I take a girl home after an evening out, I don't dump her on the area steps as if she were a Victorian housemaid,' he claimed, and knowing that, if not from her, Wilmot

86

would hear the story of her homecoming from Bran, she gave in.

At the foot of the verandah steps he took her hand. 'I'm wondering what a reluctant Blue Danube girl expects of her escort when he takes her home these days?' he said.

'Expect of him? Why, nothing—'

'No? Well, just in case, I shouldn't care to disappoint,' he said, and kissed her lightly but purposefully on her lips.

CHAPTER FOUR

Thinking over the evening, Donna realised she had had as little relish for being called a Blue Danube girl as she had for having been kissed in her escort's line of duty, because he thought she expected it. Blue Danube indeed! It was a wonder he hadn't chosen the mazurka or the gavotte if he wanted to date her dancing in the past. And since they both knew his taking her home was a chore that had been forced on him, why should he suppose she regarded him at all as someone who had invited her out and who, when he brought her home, might have kissed her goodnight when they parted?

87

Both epithet and duty kiss seemed to docket her as a type, and this she resented. In any future encounters with Mr Elyot Vance, he would have to learn that she wasn't as predictable as all that; that occasionally she could pack some surprises of temperament and mood too! (Too? All right, by 'too' her thought *had* meant 'as well as' Margot le Conte, even though her honesty had to admit that the man was right—with a mercurial spirit of that calibre her own verve and versatility would have a pretty hard job to compete. But one could always try . . .)

When she went to breakfast the next morning she found that Bran had already told her uncle about Elyot's having brought her home. 'The fellow's making a bit of a habit of it, isn't he?' Wilmot grumbled to Donna. 'Let's hope he hadn't the gall to come into my house and stay?'

'No. He just dropped me at the door and left,' Donna said.

'Good. He can evidently take a hint.' Wilmot returned to his consumption of grilled flying fish, and Donna watched Bran trying to persuade the tiny banana-quit who flew in every morning at breakfast-time to take sugar from his outstretched palm. The little bird nodded and fluttered and quirked his tail, but wasn't to be tempted. He preferred to perch on the rim of the sugar bowl and help himself.

Presently Bran said, 'Margot tells me she's enlisted you on the job as well, and that I'm to take you along with me until you've learned the ropes. Is that so?'

'Well, I hadn't given her a firm answer.' As she spoke Donna glanced in her uncle's direction, and Bran took the hint that she needed help.

'O.K. Leave it to me.' He cleared his throat loudly to call Wilmot's abstracted attention. 'Look, Dad, there's an idea afoot that as Donna ought to get around and see more of the island while she's here, she might as well come along and take a turn at driving when I go out on a tour.'

'And whose idea is it that we're not doing our duty by Donna? Is this more of the Vance fellow's interference in our affairs?' Wilmot demanded.

'Not a bit of it,' Bran assured him. 'It was Margot le Conte's suggestion, in fact. Besides, it's not a question of either of us failing Donna. You need the car and I've my job, so she couldn't expect to see much except Louvet and the town unless—' Bran paused, then took the plunge. 'Well, to be frank, the object of the exercise is that, when I've briefed her thoroughly, she might act as a stop-gap guide herself. Margot needs a woman to fall back on, you see, in case some of her timid ladies won't go out with a man. So how would you go along with that? I mean, Donna wouldn't consider it unless you agreed.'

'Though you seem to have it cut and dried between you before I've been asked to agree,' Wilmot commented, at which Donna was moved to protest, 'Miss le Conte only put it to me last night, Uncle, and to Bran when he got back to the hotel. Of course I'll go no further with it, if you'd rather I didn't. Though—'

'Though what?'

Later Donna could not have told by what flash of inspiration she had hit upon the one note likely to appeal to him when she said, 'Well, it had occurred to me that in one aspect of Miss Le Conte's idea of my "learning" Laraye, you could help me tremendously if you would. About the flowers and the trees, their names and their seasons—all that. I just wondered,' she added lamely in face of his unrelenting stare.

'And to what end, this information that you want to glean from me?' he asked.

'Just so that, if Miss le Conte ever did call on me to help her out, I could pass it on to the tourists, who, she says, want to know it all.'

'I see.' For the first time there was a gleam of interest in his cold eye. 'You get the geography from Bran and the natural science from me and feed it piecemeal to these guests of Miss le Conte's, though to whose lasting benefit, would you say?'

'Well, to mine, for one,' she retorted with spirit. '*They* can forget anything I'd been able to tell them as soon as they like. But *I* shan't. *I* want to take it all home with me—to remember and enjoy and relive as far as I can. So that's mainly why I'd like you to agree to my going out with Bran, and to helping me yourself if you will.'

'Helping you, in the time you will have, to a mere smattering of all that it's taken me a lifetime to learn, and still without having been able to put it to any rewarding purpose?' He stood up, crumpling his napkin. 'Very well. You may do as you please, which I've little doubt you would, with or without my say so—'

'I wouldn't, Uncle, really!' she disclaimed.

'And to anything you want to know what I can tell you, you're welcome.'

She smiled. 'Thank you. I'll be coming to

91

you, notebook at the ready,' she promised. But she spoke to his back as he left the verandah.

Bran said, 'Well, I congratulate myself with having conducted that with a rare turn of diplomacy.'

'You!' Donna scoffed. 'I did more than half of it, by suggesting he could help.'

'M'm—a stroke of genius, that. But who was it who had to go into action in answer to your silent, melting appeal, you tell me?'

'All right. It was you,' she conceded, then worried aloud, 'What did Uncle mean about his having achieved "no rewarding purpose" from all he knows about the Caribbean flora and fauna and all that? If you won't resent my saying so, it was the first time I'd heard him sound sad, not just sour.'

Bran nodded. 'I know. It's his pipe-dream, you see, that he's never likely to realise. He has neither the money nor many people's sympathy for his scheme for clearing part of the rain forests for a kind of natural park, with everything that's indigenous to Laraye and the other islands growing there, wild but labelled as what each specimen is. He'd see the planting of it and the care of it as the fruit of all his know-how; his gift to posterity, as it were. But it just isn't on.'

'A kind of Kew Gardens, do you mean?'

'A bit like, though wilder, and without any marked boundaries—just an acreage of the forest cleared and planted and blending with the rest. But to get it going would cost more money than we've got.'

'Aren't there any rich Larayans who would sponsor it?'

Bran shrugged. 'If there are, Dad is no salesman of anything—even of ideas.'

'Well—' Donna thought she had the solution—'there's Louvet itself, isn't there? I know it's Company owned, but as Uncle isn't making much of a success with bananas on it, and you aren't interested, mightn't the Company let him have part of it for his scheme? I could put the idea to Father, you know.'

'No dice on Louvet.' Bran shook his head. 'The conditions—soil, rainfall—aren't suitable. It's too exposed to wind and the spraying of neighbouring crops. No, it has to be further south where it's much more lush, with a lot more rain and where everything, but everything, will grow.'

'There can't be *that* difference in conditions in an island not much over thirty miles long,' Donna objected.

'Which is all you know,' Bran retorted.

'And which reminds me that you can see for yourself. I'm taking a couple down to Boiling Spring and the volcano tomorrow, and you may as well make it your first L-trip.'

There followed for Donna many days of exploration of the tortuous roads of the island—deep into the interior, east through vast banana groves to the Atlantic coast, north to fashionably developing residential estates, south through the steamy jungle of the tangled forest land, up into the mountains for views of azure blue bays far below, following the coastline through nestling fishing villages, driving to the very rim of the acrid-smelling volcano, edging along the lower shelves of gargantuan outcrops of rock which rose sheer from the sea. She surprised herself both by how much she remembered and how much she had forgotten; a scent could recall her nursery days vividly; places, such as the town park where she must often have played, meant nothing to her at all.

There was not always room for her in the car, but as larger parties usually preferred to tour together in minibuses, there often was. Bran obviously had a distinct flair for his job; he made his guide patter interesting and amusing; he was patient with questions and never grudged his passengers time to stand

and stare. Quite soon—after asking their permission—he allowed Donna to drive, at first on the easier roads, and then increasingly in the haphazard Calvigne traffic and cork-screw mountain tracks. At first she dreaded Bran's 'Here—change places with me and take over', but as she grew in confidence she became quite greedy for the time he allowed her at the steering-wheel.

She wrote home enthusiastically about this, stressing her opinion that as this, and not reluctant banana culture, seemed to be Bran's forte, he should be allowed to develop it. Of her uncle she still wrote guardedly, saying she hadn't really got through to him yet, hoping her father would remember and appreciate what a difficult man to know his brother Wilmot was.

Meanwhile she was glad that Wilmot hadn't to be reminded of his offer to identify the island's flowers for her. He lent her books of coloured prints, told her where to walk to see particular herbs and trees and the shyer flowers which didn't flaunt themselves everywhere as did the typically tropic rosy hibiscus and frangipani and anthurium, and once or twice took her further afield in his car, driving slowly and naming for her the towering forest trees, the flamboyants, the pink pouis and the cassias, and the massive fan-spread of the tree-ferns.

He knew and could relate how most of the decorative and useful growth had begun— roots and cuttings cultivated by Spanish missionaries, seeds borne in upon the relentless trade winds, orange-trees imported by the Portuguese, native yuccas and maizes and cassavas turned for use as food by Christopher Columbus. Telling all he knew on the subject he had made his own, Wilmot came alive, and Donna, interested and listening, could only suppose that his lack of enthusiasm for the banana trade was because it offered him too narrow a field. To him it was too regimented, too commercial. His true love was for all growing things, but the more wildly rampant, the better. How tragic to have your life forced into one narrow groove, when it hankered to amble gently along a wider one, she thought. And in thinking it, she decided that this was enough to have killed the man in him, the drive, the warmth—souring and deadening him into the negative figure he was. But that in this conclusion she was only partly right she was not to learn until Madame Hué erupted upon the scene.

Donna was alone and sunbathing on the

lawn one afternoon when, in an open vintage car with a strapped bonnet, Madame Hué drove down the lane at a speed conducive to hurtling herself and the car through the croton hedge and over the bluff; braked just in time, alighted and came across the lawn, both hands outstretched in greeting to Donna who had sprung to her feet in alarm, prepared for the imminent crash.

Madame Hué was small, round, dazzlingly white-haired, with a tanned face deeply creased by laughter-lines at mouth and eyes, the latter bright black buttons beneath brows which were still as black as the hair on her head was white. She announced, 'I am Irma Hué. I live on Mousquetaire Hill. I am widowed. And you are—? No, no need to tell me, except your first name. The coconut radio has already told me—you're Wilmot's niece from England. Is that not so?' Her voice grated and her accent was French.

'Yes,' said Donna, smiling. 'I'm Donna—Donna Torrence. How do you do?'

'And you will have heard of me?'

Donna hadn't, and said so.

Madam Hué clucked with annoyance. 'Bah, it is always the same with these Larayans—out of sight, out of mind, as you say. Me, I go up to Florida to visit friends—a month, two months or so—and I am forgotten until I return. Where is Wilmot? Is he at home?'

Donna said he wasn't, and offered drinks, coffee, lemon tea and a chair, all of which her visitor declined.

'No, sit down again, child, and I shall sit with you while you tell me about yourself,' she ruled, plumping down upon the lawn, sitting cross-legged and encircling her fat knees with her clasped hands to stop her rotundity from keeling over to one side or the other.

'Now,' she said. 'Now I am wearing my listening hat. And so—when did you come? Are Wilmot and Brandon entertaining you as they should? How long are you staying? And which of us all have you met yet? Have you fallen in love? Or have you left a beau— perhaps more than one—behind you in England?'

Donna laughed. 'That's quite a list of questions, Madame Hué!'

'No matter. Take your time. Let us start with the most interesting—are you in love?'

'Yes,' said Donna, and paused. 'With Laraye.'

'Bah, you tease me! You know I meant with a man,' Madame Hué accused. 'This is a romantic island, but you cannot marry an island. So tell me the names of some men to whom you have been introduced, and I, who know everyone, will tell you which one of them might make you a suitable *parti*.'

Donna's memory was able to produce the names of some of the men she had met at Margot le Conte's party, then she added. 'There's another one to whom I wasn't introduced, but just—met.'

'You—a girl of good family, and you picked him up?' Madame Hué's shocked tone was belied by the twinkle in her eye.

'Not exactly, though you could say he picked *me* up.' Donna admitted. 'At the airport, when Uncle Wilmot had mistaken the day I was arriving and hadn't met me. So he—Mr Elyot Vance—made himself known, and drove me up here on his own way home.'

'Ah,' said Madame Hué. 'Elyot Vance—what a pity.'

'A pity?'

'That you should list him among the men who have interested you.'

'You have only asked me about some I had met,' Donna pointed out.

'Yet you remember to include Elyot Vance. And so I repeat—a pity. For though he is not married, is a charmer, of about the right superior age for you, and rich, one understands that he is already registered, labelled—what is the word I want?—ah yes, *booked* to Brandon's employer, Margot le Conte of the Allamanda. So if you have an eye for Elyot, I'm afraid an *affaire* would be all you could hope for. Marriage to you would not be in his mind.'

'But I haven't! I don't—!' protested Donna, taken aback, though for some reason intrigued, rather than irritated, by these mental gymnastics on the part of her companion, who ignored her outburst to continue.

'Not that Wilmot would countenance either for you, considering how matters stand between him and Elyot. Has he—Wilmot— seen you with Elyot?'

'With him, actually only once.'

'And?'

'Well—' Finding Madame Hué an avid listener and that she herself wasn't averse to discussing Elyot Vance with a third person, Donna told the whole story of their encounters and of her uncle's reactions from beginning to end. 'It's always been sort of chance, you see,' she concluded.

Madame Hué snorted. 'Huh! Not always chance, if I know anything about Elyot's eye for a pretty girl.'

'But I'm not pretty, and it *was* chance—at the airport, and at the Dial House and when Bran couldn't drive me home. Anyway, I only mentioned him because you asked me, and because Uncle made so much difficulty about it.'

'Difficulties for which he sincerely believes he has reason.'

'Oh, I know,' Donna agreed. 'Bran told me, and we already know something about it in London—about Uncle's resentment of the competition of Marquise with Louvet, and his consequent feud with Mr Vance.'

'Which doesn't stem only from Wilmot's jealousy of Marquise; it goes much further back than that. And if you want to know how far, and what it is all about, probably only someone of Wilmot's age or of my own could tell you. I doubt if Brandon knows or would show much sympathy if he did. You young people'—the black button eyes gleamed in reproof—'you resent our generation's ever having loved or been loved. But that is what Wilmot's enmity for Elyot is all about.'

Donna was silent, suspecting she was about to hear the story, and she was right. Madame Hué continued, 'Both Elyot's parents died in the town fire of over twenty years ago.'

'Yes. He told me that,' said Donna.

'But not, one supposes, since he may not know, that almost on the eve of their wedding, his mother had broken her engagement to Wilmot and eloped with Noel Vance. They had just the one child, Elyot, and were very happy, one heard. But Wilmot never forgave Noel for taking her from him, and although Noel lost his own life in the fire, Wilmot never ceased to blame him for exposing his wife to it; Wilmot's mania ran— If she had married him, they would have been living up here in the country, safe. She would still have been alive. And even I couldn't make him see that it was all chance, and that he was wrong and vindictive to blame Noel, who died too himself.'

Donna asked, 'Uncle confided in you at the time, Madame Hué?'

'*Only* in me, I think. I was for him what you would call "the girl next door". You understand this term?'

'Yes, I think so. But he married my aunt later, and they had Bran.'

'And so did I marry too. I went away and only came back to Laraye after I was widowed. And what do I learn of my old friend Wilmot? That he is still eating out his bitter heart, not now against poor dead Noel Vance, but against his son for *being* Noel's son. But still in secret, I believe. To most people, as to your family too perhaps, it is just a business rivalry, with Wilmot always the loser. But I tell *you*, child. Do you know why? It is because when you are in danger of being a little dazzled by Elyot's empty attentions to you, in your enchantment you may side with him against Wilmot, which would be unkind of you and less than the poor embittered man deserves of his own kin.'

'But I never would! That is, I'm not *in* that kind of danger. I hardly *know* Elyot Vance,' Donna protested. 'Besides, as I told you, at our very first meeting, I defended Uncle Wilmot against him, and always would again, especially after what you have told me.'

'Then that is good, and I am sure I can trust you.' Madame Hué rocked perilously to her feet and brushed clinging crab grass from her ample trousered *derrière*. 'And now that I am back on Laraye with plans for no more trips abroad for some time, I must take Wilmot in hand myself and arrange a cure for him. A cure being a wife, which all men need.'

'He has had a wife,' Donna pointed out.

'And cherished her as he should, one hears, for all his other discontents. And so we must marry him again. I myself shall put it in train.'

'Must you go, Madame Hué? Won't you wait to see Uncle, though I can't say when he may be home?' Donna asked.

'No, I must go. Tell him I called, and you must come to see me, child.'

'How far away is Mousquetaire? I haven't a car,' said Donna.

'Then Wilmot must bring you, or Brandon, or I will fetch you myself. And call me Irma, my dear. Everyone does; I am a byword in Laraye.'

Donna laughed. 'I'm sure you're not. A byword—whatever for?'

'For minding everyone's business but my own!' With a wicked chuckle Madame Hué turned the vintage monster in its tracks and roared off up the lane, leaving Donna to pray that she would encounter no passing traffic at the top.

★   ★   ★

Bran's reaction to the news of Madame Hué's call was a laconic, 'So she's back again, is she?' and Wilmot's dour 'That woman! Did she say what she wanted of me?' sounded to Donna singularly unwelcoming to his one-time confidante.

'No. Just that she had hoped to see you,' Donna told him.

'Though as if I couldn't guess. She fancies herself as a water-colourist and has some fool idea that if I wrote a tourists' guide to the island's flowers and trees, she could do the illustrations in colour. So no doubt she came to pester me again,' Wilmot grumbled.

The idea seemed a good one to Donna, and she would have thought he would consider it. 'But you aren't interested?' she queried.

'If I ever wrote a book which I could hope any tourist would put his hand in his pocket to buy, I'd have it illustrated by someone who knew better than Irma Hué which was the right end of a paintbrush,' he ruled, dismissing the subject and causing Donna to wonder what he would say if he learned of the lady's plans, not only for a book but for a marriage of convenience for him which she intended to arrange.

How serious could she possibly have been about that? Donna wondered. Probably no more so than in her claim that Elyot Vance wasn't unwilling to allow chance to help him to add Donna's own scalp to his belt. She couldn't have meant either to be taken as fact. Donna couldn't see Wilmot ever arousing himself to marry again, and Elyot hadn't attempted to pretend he was interested . . . He had simply done what her chance emergencies had asked of him at the time. Even his peck of a goodnight kiss had been a duty chore, he had implied. And who wanted to be a mere duty to any man?

Irma Hué had not visited again by the time Bran said he had told Margot le Conte that he thought Donna was now practised enough to stand in as a spare guide whenever Margot needed her. Margot, he reported, had said, 'That's fine, the darling. But remind her that I threatened I'd put her through her paces,' and had named a day and time, which Bran had accepted for Donna.

Donna didn't relish the prospect too much. Why need Margot make it sound like the taking of one's original driving test? But on the afternoon in question a car was sent to take her down to the Allamanda, where she supposed she would be picking up Margot in one of the tourist guide cars.

On the way the Larayan driver was chatty. 'Missus le Conte she go Barbados,' he volunteered.

'Barbados? I suppose she'll be flying

down? When?' Donna asked.

He shook his head. 'No. She go today. She fly, yes. But she gone.'

Donna stared. 'Gone?'

'Thas right. Hear tell she have tooth pain bad. Say no good tooth doctor, Laraye. Doctor on Barbados better. So she go, fly back tomorrow.'

'But she had arranged to see me! She must have forgotten that.'

'No, Missus remember. Me, I know so, for I drive her airport, and as she mount car she say to Mister Vance who there, tell you not to come, as she called away. But he say he see you instead. She say no need. But he say yes, and she say—' A shrug of the man's massive shoulders indicated Margot's reply—'and Mister Vance tell me come up for you, missus, after I take Missus le Conte airport. This I do,' he concluded.

'Oh,' said Donna blankly. Stepping into the breach again, was he? She had been right to call a cliché the circumstances which forced her company upon Elyot, for his coming to her aid—quite unnecessarily this time—was indeed becoming a habit. Why, she wondered a shade irritably, had he apparently overruled Margot about putting her off? He could so easily have telephoned, and saved both the driver and her a fruitless journey.

But that he didn't intend it to be a fruitless journey was made clear when, at the hotel, she found him waiting for her in the passenger seat of one of the guide cars. He got out, and before she could tell him she already knew of Margot's emergency, he said, 'Margot has had to fly down to Barbados to see her dentist, so, rather than subject you to butterflies in the tum to no purpose, I've offered to play test-examiner myself.'

'You mean *you* want to take me round on a trial trip, as I think she meant to?' Donna asked.

'On the contrary, you're going to take *me* round.' He opened the car door for her and waited as, seeing protest was useless, she strapped herself in. As he got in beside her he produced a large-scale map of Laraye and remarked, 'You were having butterflies, I hope, as all worthy examinees should?'

'A bit,' she admitted. 'I think Miss le Conte meant to make it a serious test of what I could do.'

'Let her be "Margot" between ourselves, may we?' he said casually. 'Yes, well—' his forefinger traced a route on the map—

'around the town first, I think; points of interest there; then up to the Lighthouse; round the Military Cemetery; over to Government House. All right, I'll brief you again when we've done all that. Off you go.'

Donna moved 'off' rather nervously, over-conscious of both his scrutiny and his unreadable silences between the questions he put to her about anything of interest which they passed, not always spacing them considerately of the main task in hand—her driving of the car. He would bark, 'Look, what's that?' quite suddenly, and when she jumped and said 'What's what? Oh, that's—' and told what 'that' was, he showed no emotion at all, not even interest in her reply. But gradually she found she could interpret his every slight movement of foot or hand or clearing of his throat as some message he was putting over to her.

I'm getting on to his wavelength, she thought. *We're on the same beam*, and surprised herself at the quiet, almost warm sense of achievement which that gave her.

When he stopped her to suggest their further itinerary ('We haven't time to go full south, but drive as far as Carrière through the rain forests; on the way back, take in an avocado farm and we'll finish on Marquise') he advised, 'You're going to have to expect questions, some of them pretty fatuous, I daresay. So if you want to ward them off, you should volunteer more patter than you've offered me. Stop in your own time and hold forth about the views or whatever, and point out things off your own bat as you go.'

She did so, finding herself more at ease, even making a joke or two and repeating for her imaginary passengers' benefit some Larayan proverbs which she had learned from Juno and which amused her. She was enjoying herself; didn't want the tour to end.

At last they came down from the mountains where, on the highest roads, they had been level with the tops of the flamboyant trees and the coconut palms towering from the lower slopes. The red dust road dropped down to a valley which was the vast acreage of Marquise, one dark green mass of banana plants, with a group of Elyot's workers' cabins huddled in the middle of the mass.

He stopped Donna, told her to get out and helped her across the wide ditch which was the only barrier between the road and the growing crops. He pointed to a young plant with its pendant purple 'head' which had not yet dropped any of its bracts to reveal the tiny

110

green fingers underneath.

'Now give me a rundown on the whole banana cycle from A to Z,' he ordered.

Donna smiled. 'Doesn't that rather amount to teaching my grandmother to suck eggs?' she quipped.

'In this instance, I'm not your grandmother, thanks be. I'm a tourist straight from the heart of Chicago or Manchester who has hitherto only thought of bananas in terms of comic songs. So let's be hearing what you can tell me,' he said.

When she had finished he nodded. 'Very lucid. And the rest—the harvesting, the washing, the grading, the shipment overseas?'

'I know about it, of course. But I haven't seen it; Louvet hasn't sent out a consignment since I've been here.'

'You should rectify that. As long as you wouldn't expect me to spare you much attention, I could bring you out one banana-boat day to see the whole process through. The loading from the quays is a spectacle your passengers are sure to want to see. One thing you haven't mentioned—why, out here, the banana is known as "fig?"'

She shook her head. 'I know it is, but not why.'

'The reason is a bit involved, but it's picturesque. The plant's botanical family is Musacœ, which derives from the Arabic Mouz, and the banana, probably in its wild state one of the oldest plants known to man, appears in the Koran as the Tree of Paradise. When it first came to Europe the name held and, by association I suppose, it became the fig-tree of our Christian Garden of Eden. The Caribs are still reluctant to hear it called anything else.'

Donna murmured, 'Tree of Paradise—I like that.'

'Yes, it appeals to the romantic Eve in most women,' he agreed, then indicated the lengthening shadows cast by the plants upon the road. 'Time for sundowners, I think. Change places now, and I'll take you up to the house, where you'll meet my Maria and Choc, your Juno's relations who do for me, as Juno does for you.'

'I must deliver the car back to the hotel,' Donna reminded him.

'No hurry. When I've given you a drink, I'll take you home in it, deliver it myself and collect my own which I left down there. How's that?'

At the top of its winding driveway Marquise, unlike many houses in Volcanic

Laraye, was two-storied, with wide balconies to each floor, looking down over dipping lawns fringed by palms, and in the distance across to the sweep of the estate. Such of the interior of the house as Donna saw was beautifully furnished and be-flowered; obviously the house of a bachelor who need deny himself nothing, but still a house which any woman would be proud to be asked to share.

Choc was a mountain of a man, a full Negro. Maria was tiny, with a voice so small that Donna could hardly hear her when she asked what 'Missus' would like to drink. 'Missus' chose a fruit punch, but was persuaded by Elyot to a daiquiri. He had one too and as he took the long chair beside hers on the lower balcony, asked, 'Don't you want to know how I shall report on you to Margot?'

'Why, how will you?'

'Very favourably, I think.'

'Thank you. I've had some good teachers—Bran for the geography and Uncle Wilmot for the flower names, not to mention Juno for the Caribbean proverbs.'

'Don't I get any marks for the Tree of Paradise bit? Your passengers will fairly eat that. But it's evident that, as they say in the theatre, you're a quick study.'

'When one wants to learn anything enough it comes easily,' Donna said sincerely.

'How sententious of you! That sounds like a maxim from a copybook. But you mean Margot didn't press-gang you into it?'

'No. I'm grateful to her. I should never have got around as I wanted to, in any other way. I shall go back as full of impressions and memories as I hoped I might before I came.'

'Only to be rather let down by the reality of Louvet?'

He had no right to be so shrewd! 'A bit, perhaps,' she admitted.

'But now you'll go back happier? And you'll *go* back?'

'Of course, I've a job in England, and I shall be going home.'

'And so? Girls of your age have been known to leave home—quite a lot of them to marry in "furrin parts". Laraye, for one. I could point you to a dozen English and American girls who've married happily and successfully here.'

'I daresay. But I don't happen to have marriage in mind, here or anywhere else.'

'Oh, come! Don't tell me, when you knew you were coming to Laraye, that a tropical island and a rich planter who couldn't resist you weren't synonymous in your dreams?'

'They certainly weren't. And if they had been, they would have taken a knock. I don't know any rich planters—'

'You know me.'

'You?' Donna sat upright in such blank surprise that she spilled her drink. Elyot laughed, reached for the jug and refilled her glass.

'Take it easy. No need for a double-take of that intensity,' he teased. 'I wasn't springing a proposal of marriage, even on a couple of daiquiris. I was only quoting myself as an example of several quite well-to-do planters on Laraye who aren't married. One or two of them would like to be, I know.'

'Thank you. When I find I'm in need of a marriage bureau, I think I'll go to a real one, licensed by the London County Council. Meanwhile—'

'Meanwhile, you'll thank me not to tread on your dreams. *And* you are in a huff.'

'I'm not,' she denied, wishing he hadn't said that about treading on her dreams. It assumed too much, it was emotive and for some reason it hurt. She went on, 'This has become such a silly, hypothetical argument that it isn't worth getting huffed *about*, would you say?'

115

'*I'd* say not,' he agreed. 'But—' He didn't finish as Choc came out on to the balcony.

'Missus le Conte on telephone, suh. Want speak to you.'

'Coming.' Elyot excused himself to Donna and went back into the house.

She sat on, sipping her drink, watching the crimson-purple of the clouded sky clear slowly to the pale lemon it took on at full sundown. She knew she was a little too relaxed, not thinking very clearly. The time, the place, an early evening drink with a man had all the makings of a flirtation, she supposed hazily. So that was all their verbal sparring had amounted to—flirtation. Nothing to take seriously nor in offence. Nor even to mull over later, making more of his brittle interest in her than it deserved. They would have talked just so at a drinks party in all probability. But she still wondered why he had bothered to spare her the afternoon from his busy schedule. She would have liked to ask him, if she couldn't already foretell his bantering reply.

He came back and sat down again. 'Margot, after a nasty session with her dentist and faced by a lonely evening, in need of sympathy and moral support,' he said.

'Did you give it to her?'

'To the best of my ability from this distance. Poor Margot needs the direct touch; she suffers her own company only by dire necessity. She wanted to know whether I had done my duty by you; I reported on you as I told you I should, and said I was giving you a drink before taking you home.'

'Thank you.' Donna put down her empty glass, and then with a recklessness which only the unaccustomed drink could have encouraged, said lightly, 'Well, at least no one could accuse you of being *cinq à sept* with *me.*'

She was totally unprepared for his sudden start and the dark frown he turned on her. 'Of being *what* with you?' he demanded.

'*C-cinq à sept,*' she hesitated.

'And how on earth do you come by such a phrase?'

'I heard Miss—I mean Margot le Conte— tease you with it at her party at the hotel. I ᵤdn't know then what it meant, but I asked Bran, and he told me.'

'Well, forget it.' His tone was terse. 'Even in joke, as Margot would have used it, it hasn't the most tasteful of implications, and with reference to our afternoon together, it makes no sense at all.'

Feeling like a small child under reproof,

Donna protested, 'But that's precisely what I said just now—that it couldn't apply. It was only a joke anyway,' she added, aggrieved.

'As was Margot's. All right, leave it.' He let the silence lengthen into one minute, two. Then, just as Donna was about to suggest she would like to go home, he voiced aloud the question she had been asking herself. 'Haven't you wondered why I volunteered to act as Margot's stand-in today?'

Her eyes met his frankly. 'Yes,' she said, 'I had. It seemed so unnecessary that you should.'

He shook his head. 'I needed to talk to you, and since I'm *persona non grata* in your uncle's house, this was the first chance I'd had of getting you alone.'

'To talk to me?' Donna's mouth went dry and there was a flutter of excitement in the region of her heart. 'What about?'

'This,' he said. 'Listen—'

CHAPTER FIVE

For a long time afterwards Donna was to cringe inwardly at the thought of her hope that it was some personal confidence, some small intimacy, which Elyot had wanted to share with her alone. For what he had to say was so much an anti-climax that she wondered with shame whether her disappointment had shown in her face.

'It's about the Dial House,' he said.

'The—Dial House?' She knew her surprise sounded blank.

'Yes. My ultimatum fell flat. Your uncle hasn't done anything about it, has he?'

'About repairing it? No. After the way you and he parted, did you expect him to?'

'Frankly no. That's where you come in, and why I needed to get you alone.'

'*I* can't force him.'

'I realise that, but I want you as a fellow-conspirator. I suggest that you make an urgency of it to your father, asking him that the Company should bypass your uncle and make a direct ruling as to the repair of the place.'

'But in writing home I haven't mentioned it at all.'

'Why not?'

'Because—well, I suppose I was ashamed of my foolhardiness that first day, and I didn't want to worry them.'

'Nor admit to the hornets' nest you stirred up, Louvet versus Marquise-wise?'

119

'That too, though they know something about that. But if I did appeal to Father, and the Company did act, Uncle Wilmot would guess what I'd done, even that you'd put me up to it.'

'Why should he?' Elyot parried. 'He must realise that the Company knows what property it owns, and if you enlist your father on your side, your uncle could be led to suppose it had been decided at company level that it was time the Dial was put in repair, with or without his consent.'

'Mm, perhaps,' Donna mused. 'But wouldn't that be riding a bit roughshod over him?'

'Roughshod? In the interest of my workers' toddlers, not to mention the risk of the whole crazy structure collapsing like a pack of cards, come the hurricane season? Thank you, but I'm not going to get any satisfaction from chanting "I told you so" if or when it happens. So if you won't co-operate, I'll write to your Company myself.'

'I will, of course,' Donna promised reluctantly, though having known all the time that she must.

'Good girl! I knew I could trust you. And one other thing—since I'm an extremely interested party, I'd like you to mention that

I'd supply the planning and the labour, as I said in the first place I would.'

Donna shook her head. 'Uncle would never wear that.'

Elyot laughed. 'Don't put goat mout' 'pon it—which, on the parallel that a goat can destroy anything with his nibbling, is vulgar Larayan for "Don't crab the chances of success." If the Company accept the reason for my offer, and the whole operation comes as a directive from them, what can the man do?'

Donna smiled thinly. 'Be difficult,' she said. 'At the very least.'

'And at the very most? He's already forbidden me his house, yet I survive.'

She did not answer, not wanting to look at an immediate future which Wilmot could make quite untenable for her if he chose to forbid her to see even as little of Elyot as she had done until now. To a guest, while she remained under his roof, Wilmot had the right to do that. Yet the prospect of no more contacts with Elyot appalled her. Which meant—?

It meant, she realised after they had parted that evening, that by some emotional about-face she had thought never to experience where he was concerned, his challenge to her,

121

their frictions as well as their agreements, were becoming important, too important. And not only his challenge. The physical man himself—manner, voice, movement—all the dynamic virility she had sensed at her first stranger's awareness of him—had begun to matter too much. He was too often in her thoughts; in the expectation with which she woke each morning to the little secret question, dismissed at once, of 'Am I likely to see him today?' An on-the-brink-of-love question, that. Her feminine instinct knew the signs, but hadn't warned her against caring whether the answer had to be yes or no.

How had it happened? That other time of their parting at night she had resented the spirit in which he had kissed her; this evening she would have made treasure of it, however little he meant by it. But he had not kissed her. On his own admission he had only wanted to see her today in order to enlist her help. So what had her hunger for his interest to feed upon? Just that he had said he trusted her enough to know he could look to her as an ally. But that was all. At best, she was only on the fringe of his life. And on the fringe of her own was where, if she were wise, she would learn to keep him. If she were wise . . .

She wrote fully to her father about the Dial House, admitting now her own escapade, relating Elyot's timely rescue of her, and telling of the subsequent violent clash between him and her uncle on the matter of its repair. She emphasised Elyot's understandable concern for it, and suggested that he be contacted directly, if the Company could see its way to falling in with his plan.

She was still awaiting a reply to this when Margot called her to her first guide tour.

Over the telephone Margot gushed, 'Darling, Elyot gave you the full thumbs-up over your driving. *So* gallant of him to save me the bore of going out with you myself, and sweet of you to help me out. Now I have for you an advertising woman who is collecting copy about the Caribbean; if you get on together, may I assign you to her for later trips she may want to make? O.K.?'

Though she went to her first appointment in some trepidation Donna enjoyed it herself and was thanked, congratulated and re-booked by her client, an Englishwoman intent on selling Laraye and its sister islands in rivalry to the more popular West Indian resorts.

There followed other pleasant assignments. Donna found herself in demand by the hotel's women tourists needing a guide, and she was expecting nothing unusual when she went down one day to keep an appointment with two American ladies, newly arrived overnight.

They were not waiting for her outside, nor in the foyer, which was empty but for a man who at first was chatting to the girl desk-clerk, then idly scanning the bookstand between glances at his watch. Donna returned to her car to wait for her passengers, but when they had not appeared after another ten minutes, she went back into the foyer to check with the clerk.

'Mrs and Miss Bellew, Rosa—have you seen them waiting for me?' she asked.

Rosa shook her head. 'Don't know lady that name.'

'You might not. They are new guests. But anyway, two ladies whom I was to take on a tour?'

Light dawned for Rosa. 'Oh—yes, two ladies. But they go with Louis just now.'

'With Louis? But they were my passengers, and I wasn't late.'

'I send them with Louis, all same. I think

that right. This gentleman for you, mebbe yes, Missus Torrence? Perhaps he wait for someone drive him,' Rosa said hopefully.

Donna shook her head. Margot had never engaged her for a man passenger; that hadn't been in their arrangement. 'Not for me, I think,' she said. But the man was already at her side, smiling and saying, 'But as there seems to have been some mix-up, you'd take me, I daresay? I'd be honoured if you would. Take pity on me, won't you, and say yes— *please*?' His accent was American with a drawling Southern inflection, he was darkly handsome in what she thought of as a film-star way, and his ready smile invited hers.

She hesitated, her native caution none too willing to drive him alone. In order to gain time for decision, she told Rosa, 'I'd better look at the bookings ledger' and while she did so, checking that the Bellews were indeed rightly her passengers and that no man on his own was booked for that hour at all, she sensed Rosa's worry over the mistake, and made up her mind to help the girl out.

'Very well,' she told the man. 'Since I seem to be free, I'll drive you. Where would you like to go?'

He held out his hand. 'Thanks a million. Anywhere, everywhere. I was hoping to fix up something, but I didn't expect—' His glance was openly admiring of her as he went on, 'Names, first? I'm Mel, short for Melford. Who are you?'

'Donna *Torrence*.' She laid deliberate emphasis on her surname, and he laughed. 'O.K., hint taken, Mel *Drinan*—will that do? But does all the heavy stress mean that we're not to be Mel and Donna as we go on our way? *Mr* Drinan and *Miss* Torrence—it *is* Miss, and not Mrs, I hope?'

'It's Miss.' Donna relented. 'I only mean that I don't usually call people by their first names, until I'm asked.'

'As I'm asking you and warning you I'm going to call you Donna. Pretty name, Donna, a gift. Does that mean your people saw you as rather a special gift when they named you?'

'I shouldn't think so,' she said, remembering her father's prejudice in favour of a son, but doubting whether this readily amiable young man would appreciate the Dickens reference as Elyot had done. *Elyot*! By contrast with his blunt demanding approach, this one's was positively honey-tongued! 'You are American, aren't you?' she asked him.

'Uh-huh. From Houston, Texas. But to

save your asking, I'm not in oil. I'm in real estate, prospecting for possible developments on Laraye. And you are English, of course?'

'Yes.' As he took the passenger seat beside her, she asked again, 'Where would you like to go? If you are interested in housing, perhaps you would like to see the development that has been done already in the north of the island?'

'No hurry,' he said easily. 'Unless of course it's on the way to anywhere particularly romantic that you fancy yourself. Take me there and let me share it, won't you, please?'

'It would help me to plan a route, if you would say how long you would like to be out,' she told him, and he waved an airy hand.

'Just as long as you can spare for me. Do you have another fare after this?'

'No.'

'Well then, let's play it by ear. *I've* got all day. Meanwhile I'm counting my luck that you didn't have to pick up those two dames. Let's go.'

By no means averse to showing off her driving skill, she chose the most tortuous road into the mountains which she knew, offering him sea-views and inland panoramas and a patter of folklore in her best professional vein. She realised, from his reference to her 'fares' and his questions to her about the job and whether it paid, that he thought she did it for a living, and it amused her not to disillusion him.

She lived out in the country, she told him, on a not very prosperous banana estate, part-owned and managed by her uncle. Her cousin also acted as a guide-driver for the Allamanda. And yes, she enjoyed her work, and no, so far she hadn't had any 'difficult' clients.

When, at around noon, they dropped down to the coast and she drove through a succession of fishing villages nestling in the lee of beetling cliffs, his interest in various restaurants they passed told her that he was thinking in terms of luncheon and perhaps debating whether to suggest her joining him.

At last he made up his mind. 'Would it be in order for you to lunch with me?' he asked.

'Thank you. I think so,' she said demurely.

'Then where?'

She took him to a quiet restaurant, palm-shaded, on the very edge of the shore, where she knew the seafood to be excellent and the service unobtrusive. But when he didn't approve it, saying it looked a bit tatty to him, she went to the other extreme and drove to one of the newer hotel-restaurants catering for tourists, where the guests were lodged in pseudo-Tahitian thatched cabins on the beach, from where the dining-room was reached by cable car up the mountainside. This her companion liked, though she thought it rather ostentatious. At the bar she chose a soft drink as she was driving, and took only half a glass of the bottle of wine he ordered with the meal, leaving the rest to him.

They talked. He told her he would be taking a few days' holiday before getting down to his firm's assignment to him to prospect for available building land and negotiate its price. As soon as he started work in earnest, he would be hiring a car himself, but in the meanwhile, perhaps she would take him out again? And when he had his own car he would hope for some dates with her. *Might* he hope?

She agreed guardedly, keeping up the fiction that she was not entirely a free agent while, though he talked about himself and his work, she learned nothing personal about him nor his background. Meanwhile, he was pleasant company and never lost an opportunity for a compliment, either oblique or direct. Everything about his appearance spoke of affluence—pale lilac silk shirt, impeccable grey slacks, casually knotted Charvet neckerchief, broad signet ring of plain gold—leading her to conclude that he was probably at executive level in what sounded like a very prosperous firm, though, in keeping with his reticence about his personal affairs, he hadn't told her its name.

On the drive back his manner became more intimate and his attention more concentrated on her as she talked than on what she was telling him about the scenery they were passing. Once he slid an arm across the back of her seat, but when she sat slightly forward, showing she knew it was there and that it irked her, he withdrew it at once. 'Sorry,' he smiled disarmingly. 'Getting cramp in that elbow; just flexing the muscles, that was all,' which was so adroit a retreat from what might or might not have been a tentative pass that she gave him the benefit of the doubt with her concerned, 'Oh dear—is it better now?'

At the hotel he thanked her warmly and made an embarrassed gesture towards his wallet. At first she thought, horrified, that he was going to offer her a tip, but when he asked, 'Whom and how does one pay?' she told him she would put in a chit and the cost

130

would appear on his account.

'Fine,' he said. 'And now, could we have a swim in the pool and an early drink before you go home?'

Donna refused. She didn't keep a swimsuit at the Allamanda and besides—a white lie—she had an appointment to see Miss le Conte, the owner-manageress, before she left, she told him.

'Dinner, then? Tonight? Tomorrow?' he pressed. 'Here, or wherever you like instead?'

She hesitated. A dinner date for which she could dress up would be nice, and though she had taken to him only moderately, the man was no wolf. But though she had no appointment with Margot, she had meant to find what were Margot's reactions to her having taken out a man passenger alone and, now that he had asked her, how Margot would view her acceptance of his invitation to dine. So she said she wasn't sure about the evening, but she would ring him—with which he seemed satisfied, and after he had named a time, they parted.

Rosa, questioned as to where Margot might be, said she was in her apartment. Donna said, 'Well, ring her for me, will you please, and ask her if she can spare me a few minutes?'

Rosa's brown eyes widened. 'You not make trouble wid Missus le Conte 'bout dem two ladies?' she pleaded.

'Of course not,' Donna assured her. 'Are they back yet? How did they get on with Louis?'

'Dey say super. Fine.' Rosa was beaming now. 'Louis great chap, dey say; good type, want him again. Ring Missus le Conte now; tell her you here.'

After a minute or two she reported, 'Missus say she occupied; she dressing, but if you won't keep her long, you go up.'

Margot was in her opulent bedroom. Clad in a frilled silk negligée, she was doing her nails at the dressing-table; a valise, half packed, was open on the bed.

She spoke to Donna over her shoulder while fanning out her fingers to see the effect of a silver pearl polish. 'You find me terribly pressed, darling—just half an hour before Elyot Vance calls for me. He has to go to Grenada on business by the evening plane; staying the night, and I'm going along for the ride; back tomorrow. Was it anything madly important you wanted?'

'Not so very,' Donna said. 'It's just that the Mrs Bellew and her daughter who were

132

booked to me this morning thought they were supposed to go with Louis Trapontine, and went. That left me without a passenger, so I took instead a Mr Drinan, who hadn't booked, but wanted a tour. Was that all right?'

'You took him alone?'

'Yes—on a pretty comprehensive drive. He gave me luncheon. Was all that in order?'

'In order? But of course, darling. You should know me—I never turn down business, and if you were free and felt you could handle him, why not? Anyway, who did you say he was? There was such a crowd of new people in yesterday.'

'His name is Drinan—Melford Drinan.'

Margot turned then. 'Melford *Drinan?*' she echoed. 'Well, what d'you know? I knew he'd booked in, but I haven't seen him yet. So aren't you the canny girl to leap to his aid? For I suppose he told you who he is—one of *the* Drinan family of Houston, who trade as Hexagon Development Inc—just about the major land prospectors in the States? Florida, Bermuda, Jamaica—you name it, and wherever there's real estate to be negotiated, Hexagon will be there. So if you made any kind of a hit with Melford Drinan, cultivate him, do. He could be well worth your while.

Did he say he would like you to drive him again?'

'Until he hires a car of his own, he said, and he asked me to dine with him tonight or tomorrow. I said I would let him know.'

'So go ahead. What are you waiting for? Make it here tomorrow night; it's a gala evening and more fun than just dining. And what did I tell you—that this way you would meet people? Men, of course I meant, because you English girls who used to get yourselves invited out to India to find husbands now holiday in the West Indies with the same idea. And why not, bless you? It's a universal game, and all of it good for the tourist trade.'

'Some of us come out for different reasons from that,' Donna observed, her tone dry.

Margot shook her head. 'You don't fool me. You wouldn't be human if you didn't keep one eye lifting in that direction—'

She broke off as the telephone rang. 'Excuse me.' She reached for the receiver. 'Ah—Elyot.' Her deep voice made a caress of the name. 'Yes—coming. Almost at once. Just must *throw* on a clout and *fling* a few more things into my case. While you're waiting, have them send a boy up for it, will you? What's that? I know... I know, but

134

I've been delayed a bit by—guess who? Your young protegée, Donna Torrence. And guess what, too? She's on the verge of hooking herself a prize fish—Melford Drinan of Hexagon Inc—*you* know, and she came to ask if it was all right for her to encourage him. Isn't that sweet? Too utterly *ingénue* for words! Been out with him for hours today; dining with him tomorrow. Yes, all right, she's leaving this minute, and I'll be down. 'Bye, monster—' She turned with a smile to Donna. 'You don't mind if I have to rush you, honey, do you? I just had to tell Elyot that you've found yourself a boy-friend— relieve him a bit of having to look after you as he has done to date. But now I must *dash*. Good luck with the date, and be sure to keep me posted, won't you? I adore watching love-affairs burgeon; at the beginning they're so naïve!'

'It isn't a—' But Donna wasn't allowed to finish. Margot's hands, gently, but firmly at her back, propelled her from the room.

★   ★   ★

There could have been several reasons why she told Melford Drinan that she would have dinner with him that night, rather than the next. It might have been sheer contrariness; or that, in asking Wilmot for the loan of his car to drive herself down to the hotel, she couldn't wait to assure him, in answer to his growled, 'You'll be bumping into that fellow Vance again, I suppose,' that she knew Elyot to be away, and that her date was with someone else. But at heart she knew it was because she couldn't bear the thought of Margot's goldfish-bowl scrutiny of her evening in Melford Drinan's company. She could just hear Margot patronising her; even enlarging on the theme of Elyot's alleged responsibility for her. As if he had ever felt any in depth! Whatever he had done for her had been thrust upon him, and the only time he had sought her out voluntarily he had wanted something of her. No, she felt she would like to tell Margot, as far as obligations were concerned, honours between her and Elyot were easy.

Meanwhile, throughout that first evening with Melford, her thoughts were following Elyot and Margot to Grenada; intimately together in the little island plane, staying in the same hotel. They must both be too well known to risk scandal, but their rooms might not be far apart. They would dance during dinner and Margot would make a spectacle of it with the same abandon she always brought to dancing to the insistent beat and rhythm of a West Indian band. They would talk. If Margot enlarged on Donna's alleged 'catch', would Elyot be interested? And if he were meeting the friend he had been seeing off to Grenada at the airport that first day, would he remember to relate how the 'And Son' of Torrence And Son had turned out to be the mosquito-beset girl who had overheard every word of his disparagement of Wilmot and Bran? Or had he already forgotten the incidents of a day which to her had marked her first sight and awareness of him, yet which for him was just an ordinary one in his calendar, without special importance at all?

She went out with Melford Drinan several times after that. Whatever his business interests on Laraye, he seemed to be master of his own time, and when he hired a car for himself, he asked her often to lunch or dine or for drinks and a swim. He was punctilious with chocolates or flowers, and when, on parting from her at night, he expected to kiss her, she let him. Unlike Elyot, he didn't claim it as a duty he owed her expectations of him, and while she was light-years away from its meaning anything to her, and he saw it as a pleasant way of bringing an evening to a close, why not?

Since their first date they hadn't always met at the Allamanda, giving Donna to hope that, by spreading their patronage to other hotels and swimming-pools, Margot would be deprived of capital for gossip to Elyot or to anyone else.

But they were due for dinner at the Allamanda on the day that Wilmot received a letter from the Company, committing him, at the Company's expense, to the immediate repair of the Dial House, the condition of which had been adversely reported upon in strong terms by Mr Elyot Vance of the Marquise estate, whose concern for the public danger was such as to cause him to offer both his own architect's services and the necessary labour for the restoration of the property—which offer the Company had been grateful to accept; and had so informed Mr Vance by current airmail, understanding that as soon as he received the Company's agreement he would put the work in hand.

While Donna read the letter which Wilmot had handed to her, he was echoing aloud some of its formal phrases which he seemed to find particularly offensive.

'"Strong terms." "Concern for the public danger." The wheeling and dealing of the fellow! Knew the Growers' Association couldn't give him the go-ahead to interfere, so he creeps behind my back to get a ruling from the Company which he knows I can't ignore!'

Donna returned the letter, grateful for her father's tact in keeping her name out of the affair. 'Mr Vance did give you the opportunity to act with him yourself, without his going to the Company,' she reminded Wilmot. 'On the same terms too—that he would undertake the actual work.'

'Under threat that he would go to the Company if I didn't agree. That's blackmail, no less! Does he realise, I'd like to know, that every man-jack he puts on the job will be a trespasser on my property?'

'I'd doubt that, if he has our Company's permission to put them there.'

'Bah! And I suppose he'll expect me to be grateful to him for doing it?'

'And I should doubt that too,' said Donna. 'He didn't sound very much bothered about getting your approval, and since he has gone over your head, I can't think he will look to you for an about-face on something he'll be doing for his own satisfaction.'

It was difficult, this sitting on a peace-fence between the two men. Previously, after

Madame Hué's visit, Donna had asked Bran what, if anything, he knew of the deep causes for Wilmot's antagonism for Elyot. But Bran, sceptical and only vaguely interested, had proved Madame Hué's contention that the younger generation did not easily appreciate that its elders could love or suffer for love, and it was left to Donna, seeing both sides through the eyes of loyalty and dawning love, to wish she dared say to either man—'Enough is enough, and it's all been water under the bridge for a long, long time.' But which of them was likely to listen to her if she did?

Sometimes on their dates Melford Drinan would call for her. Usually, when they were to meet at the Allamanda, she would drive down herself in Wilmot's car, and she did so that evening. They were to rendezvous in the salon adjoining the main bar. She couldn't see him when she arrived, so as there was a great crush there, she found a seat fairly near the door, in order to intercept him as soon as he came in.

She saw him before he saw her. As he came through the open swing doors abreast of several other people, Donna's glance went beyond him to notice Elyot not far behind him. She looked back at Melford and moved towards him, getting ready to smile a greeting. But he came on, seeing her, she knew from his direct look at her, but giving no sign of recognition; instead making some observation to the tall, ash-blonde girl beside him, who in turn passed it on to the exquisitely groomed, statuesque woman on her other side.

The three laughed, and Donna, seeing Melford's solicitous hand beneath the girl's elbow, halted so suddenly that she was jostled by someone behind her.

So they hadn't just happened to be level at the doorway. The two woman were *with* Melford, and in consequence he had cut her dead! That he was not alone had to be the reason, for Donna was quite certain he had seen her. Moreover, when she allowed them to pass within a yard or two of her on their way into the salon, he had looked at her again, his eyes vacant as a stranger's.

She couldn't believe it. It was an experience she had never suffered before. She stood as if rooted, a lone island of a figure around whom people had to divide. She felt waves of mortification and anger flood hot colour into her face. Had anyone who knew her seen her humiliation, she wondered—and found the question answered when a hand clamped about her wrist, holding it low, out of sight of those around her, and she found herself staring into Elyot's blazing eyes.

Almost through clenched teeth he muttered, 'We're getting out of here. Come—'

'What—?' She pulled against him, but his grip on her wrist was like a handcuff as he shouldered a way for himself and for her, out through the doors, across the bar and taking the opposite direction from the car-park, drew her the whole length of the adjoining colonnade to a point where it was deserted and shadowed.

There he released her, freeing her with so abrupt a turn of his own wrist that she was flung round to face him. 'So,' he accused her thickly, 'it took *that*, did it, to show you how the drip regards you? As a pretty pass-the-time at best, and at worst, only just this side of a common call-girl—!'

At that she flared, and her open palm only failed to make violent contact when he caught her hand within an inch of his cheek, and jerked it back at her.

'That was vixenish and kitchenmaid. Don't do it again,' he warned her.

'You called me something worse than a kitchenmaid!' she flashed.

'Well, was I wrong to conclude you've let yourself be treated so? Just now you *were* ready to greet the guy with a wreathed smile—right?'

'We—we had a date for dinner,' she said faintly.

'And he meant you to get the message that he didn't want to know, being otherwise engaged—right again?'

'He cut me deliberately—yes.'

'Spelling it out that, as I've said, you've been nothing better than a fill-gap for his leisure all these weeks. Or do you deny that he's only had to beckon, and you've gone running? Dinner, lunch, drinks—you name it. Well?'

'It hasn't been like that. He has asked me out quite often, but I haven't always gone.'

'No? I'll believe you if you can name six occasions when you've turned him down.'

'There haven't *been* many more than six times in all. And anyway, how would you know if there had?' she demanded with a false bravado of a child caught out in a lie.

'Oh, my dear—!' His tone was mock-pitying of her naîveté. 'Haven't you learnt yet the extent to which, in a tight little community like Laraye, we *all* know *all* that goes on, and anything we happen to miss,

143

someone is bound to tell us, whether we're interested or not?'

'In other words you, not interested, as you were, couldn't escape hearing about me and Melford Drinan?'

'If no one else told me, Margot would have done. As Nature abhors a vacuum, she abhors uneven numbers among the sexes, and getting them neatly matched up, two by two, is by no means the least of her many, many talents. A pity she seems to have been wrong about Drinan's pursuit of you being for real; her instinct for romance doesn't usually betray her like that, but she may have been misled by the stars in your eyes, perhaps.'

'There haven't *been* stars in my eyes for him!'

'There were tonight when you looked at him. Who is your glamorous rival, do you know?'

Donna shook her head. 'I've never seen her before.'

'Nor the social dragon type with her? Her mother? An aunt? No matter. We'll find out. And now—what for you?'

'Now? I shall go straight home, of course.'

'Run away and hide and lick your wounds? You'll do no such thing. You'll dine here—

144

and like it.'

'Alone? In full view, when you say everyone knows?'

'You'll dine—with me. And what's more, you'll be *seen* to like it.'

'I—can't. You'll be dining with Margot.'

'Margot has joined a party on board the banana boat for dinner. I dropped in for a drink and wasn't staying for dinner. I shall now, so come along and show some spirit. You aren't the first girl to be taken for a ride, and you won't be the last. So come.'

At the entrance to the dining-room he took some time choosing a table, even consulting the head waiter's chart before accepting a centrally-placed one where he seated Donna facing the whole room before he excused himself for leaving her while he telephoned Choc to say that he wouldn't be dining at home. He was away for some time, and while he was gone a waiter showed Melford Drinan and his guests to a table apart from Donna's by only a few yards, leaving her in little doubt as to the reason for Elyot's choice and his insistence on seeing the table plan. He had meant to embarrass Melford with her proximity and he couldn't have chosen better; already Melford was avoiding looking in Donna's direction, and it was going to be

145

difficult for him to glance about him in any natural way at all if he were not to catch her eye while she was so near.

Elyot came back. As he sat down he announced, 'Latest arrivals—Mrs Clara Berger and her daughter Ingrid; the latter, fiancé of Melford Drinan of Hexagon Inc.; the two ladies having descended on him unheralded, to surprise him for his birthday.'

Donna drew a sharp breath. 'How—how do you know?'

He shrugged. 'Reception desks know everything and will tell it all for a small fee. And now—if it hurts like nobody's business and as if your life depended upon it—*smile*?'

Donna smiled, and wished she could tell him why it didn't hurt a bit.

CHAPTER SIX

Since she was more angry than hurt, and it was only her pride that was in shock, Donna found she could despise Melford Drinan's efforts to ignore her. What a snob and a coward the man was! Though—her scorn checked guiltily on the thought—wasn't she perhaps equally a coward to have let Elyot force his protection on her in order to save her face with Melford? Oughtn't she to have had the dignity to refuse his offer of shelter?

In fantasy she saw herself doing it—drawing upon hauteur to tell him something like, 'If you think *that* of me, you can't want to be seen with me, except from pity, which I don't need.' That would at least have been in keeping with her primitive impulse to slap his face for his insult.

But somehow fantasy couldn't stand up to the hard fact of his dominance; of his refusal to be thwarted in any purpose he saw as right. He thought she needed moral support against Melford; he meant to afford it, and from experience Donna had learned that a No to his will was not a word he would tolerate. Not that—for quite other reasons than he would understand—had she really wanted to say No . . .

During dinner he made a business of his attentions to her—ordering for her an orchid spray from the flower-girl, calling acquaintances over to be introduced or for chat between courses and inviting her to dance whenever Melford and his fiancée were also taking the floor. And since only Donna knew that the show was staged merely for Melford's discomfiture, she wondered how the story of Elyot's elaborate entertainment of her would reach Margot's ears.

Would the gossips make capital of it— (When the cat is away . . .) or would Elyot relate it and its reasons to Margot himself? And would Margot agree magnanimously that it had been the least he could do for darling Donna in face of so blatant a snub? Donna viewed the latter prospect with distaste. Elyot had acted tautly and promptly on his pity for her; Margot would make such a meal of hers!

At the end of the evening Elyot insisted on seeing her home.

'That's not necessary,' she told him. 'I drove myself down in Uncle Wilmot's car.'

'Mean to say our two-timing friend hasn't been calling for you on dates and taking you home?'

'Not when I was able to borrow the car.'

'As I might have guessed. Sultan summons his current favourite houri and she hastens to his command. And when you had wined and dined or whatever, he saluted you chastely in the car park and waved you away?' Evidently concluding—rightly—that she would scorn to answer this, he went on, 'Where are you parked? I'll get one of the hotel drivers to ferry your car back, and I'll drive you in mine.'

Having yielded to him on the major issue, Donna felt this was too minor a one for argument. She indicated her car, saw him approach a man, watched money pass, and then Elyot was handing her into his own car.

Donna never ceased to marvel at the magic of the island by night. It had been raining earlier, and as they skirted the town the pavements shone cleanly and the street lamps wore nimbuses of gold in the humid air. The lights on the quays cast broken paths across the water of the harbour; music and laughter came from the open doors of taverns, and the residential hills were dotted with domestic lights to a certain level, above which the heights were uniformly black. It was not until the last house had been left behind and they were into the dark of the forest trees and not now very far from Louvet, that Elyot remarked, 'Well, I hope the exercise has done something for your self-respect. But what are you going to do when the fellow comes creeping to apologise?'

'If this evening was anything to go by, he isn't going to look my way long enough to apologise,' Donna said.

'But if he does, are you going to let him get away with explaining he had grit in his eye,

and chant, "Not to worry. All is forgiven"?'
Elyot persisted.

'Which would get me a long way, wouldn't
it, in face of a life-sized fiancée with a prior
claim?' she retorted.

He glanced at her quickly. 'Was that the
voice of cynicism, or of wounded resignation
to your having been conned'

'Neither. Just accepting the fact that a very
pleasant interlude is over.' Donna's tone was
dry.

'There wasn't much "acceptance" in your
face when he cut you dead!'

'Because I didn't care for the way it was
done. But there's no question of his deceiving
me. We both enjoyed each other's company,
but that was as far as it went.'

'By his will or yours? All right, you don't
have to answer that. To my reading of it, that
look on your face said it all.'

'Said *what* all?'

'That you were looking at a man you had
begun to care about, and couldn't believe he
could treat you so. With cause, I daresay,
because between his allowing you to
chauffeur yourself to your rendezvous and
bidding you goodnight, no doubt he made
love to you?'

'It depends on what you mean by making

love.'

'You know perfectly well what we mean by it these days, and it isn't your chap manoeuvring to hold your hand after he's picked up your dropped fan. Presumably he kissed you?'

'I don't have to answer that either!'

Elyot laughed. 'My dear, you've answered it by refusing to. And if it was all so platonic, why was he guilty enough to hand you the frozen mitt?'

Sensing that he saw that as unanswerable, Donna said nothing. She realised too the futility of suggesting that he drop her at the top of the lane to the house, and when he reached it he drove down it in silence and stopped the car.

'Thank you.' She stirred in her seat and bunched her long skirts preparatory to getting out. But when he made no move himself she added, 'Thank you too for thinking you had to come to my rescue; I do admit I'd never been cut so deliberately before, and for the moment I *was* shattered.'

He shrugged. 'Feel free to appeal for a repeat performance any time,' he said.

'There won't be another time.'

'Meanwhile you enjoyed our evening?'

'Very much.'

'Good. So there only remains some unfinished business—'

She turned her head quickly, looking a question to which her senses knew the answer. For his arms were round her, his head bent, his lips too close to hers for any intent other than the long searching kiss they extorted, urging a submission she was tempted to yield to the reality of his nearness, his touch, the warmth of his breath on her cheek, the pressure of his hold. This ought to be a dream come true... But 'unfinished business'! Making a duty of kissing her, and expecting her compliance because she had admitted her gratitude for all the rest!

No. She didn't think she had uttered the word aloud, but whether or not, as she stiffened within his arms he held her off from him, his wry scrutiny measuring her reaction.

'That was totally unnecessary,' she said.

'Unnecessary? What a dreary word! Anyway, whoever kisses a girl of necessity?' he parried. 'I can think of a dozen reasons for, and necessity's not one of them. Competition, for instance—'

Her heart quickened, but she mustn't let herself believe it. 'You're not in competition for me against anyone,' she snapped.

'For this evening's you, I am. Against

friend Drinan. When a guy has been allowed to cut in, you shouldn't underrate his urge to do better than the other fellow. Matter of male pride, you might say, and a really co-operative girl would indulge it.'

'*Would* she? Would she indeed?' Donna raged. 'Indulge him in something completely pseudo, just to boost his ego, or—maybe—to do a Tommy Tucker act in payment for her supper?'

His hands, still holding her lightly, dropped away. 'If I may say so, that was well below the belt,' he remarked.

She knew it and regretted it, but couldn't bring herself to apologise. Instead she murmured lamely, 'You can hardly blame me for wondering—'

'On the contrary, I can and I do. I told you I kissed you just now for competition's sake, and however shady you consider that, it's not as low as expecting payment for services rendered. Anyway, forget it. You can quit wondering from now on. It won't happen again,' he retorted, his dismissive tone a rebuke she couldn't take.

Making that his exit line, was he? Well, she had one to deliver too. 'With me, perhaps not,' she said. 'But tomorrow night, with another girl, in competition with another man? And the night after that—' She checked, daunted by the ironic lift of his brows.

'*Three* different girls inside a week?' he mocked. 'Promiscuous opportunist I may be, but that's achievement indeed!'

Later Donna was to realise that if she had accepted that as lightly as he said it, she might have laughed with him and they would have parted friends. But at the moment she was too hurt, too disillusioned, too cheated of dreams. She had to hit back.

'Is it so very much more than your reputation says of you?' she queried, and then added the unforgivable thing. 'It isn't as if, either, you were all that free to play around, competing. There's—Margot', she said.

His immediate answer to that was to open the door on his side, go round and open hers. He helped her out and with a hand beneath her elbow, marched her to the foot of the verandah steps, where he said, 'You can leave Margot out of this, do you mind? Goodnight.'

He didn't wait to see her into the house, and as she watched him return to the car without looking back her heart was crying, 'Fool! Fool! He kissed you, wanted to, even

154

if only just for tonight. And you could have tried to understand, even gone along with him in that spirit, enjoyed it, however little real promise it had for you. Instead—'

But the Instead was so shame-making that she couldn't bear to recall it. *Blot it out. Forget it. Think of something else.*

She only wished she could. It had lost her a friend.

★   ★   ★

She suffered a restless night, but daylight brought more balance, more detachment, and she was able to persuade herself that the situation was not all of her making. She had been goaded into her spiteful mud-slinging, and if only in return for Elyot's initial contemptuous name-calling—which showed what he really thought of her?—she could almost justify it.

Admittedly it wasn't the done thing, to taunt a man about his reputation with women, nor to accuse him of exacting payment in return for his hospitality. But Elyot had asked for it—hadn't he?—by kissing her in the intense way he had, tempting her to believe in its promise, and then claiming it as the unfinished business of proving himself the better man of two!

Donna's veering from her overnight mood of self-blame and regret was so complete that from there she went on to wonder whether Elyot too might be having second thoughts. Perhaps he would telephone. He might want her to know that he had had the green light from the Company to go ahead with the restoration of the Dial House. Or he might just ring to say Hello, How goes it?—which he would intend as face-saving for them both. Or he might be there, and normally friendly, the next time she went down to the Allamanda.

But he was not there. He did not ring on any pretext. He gave no sign of having anything more to say to her or to do with her at all.

Meanwhile events proved him wrong in his forecast of a situation where Melford Drinan would excuse his conduct to Donna and she might be weak enough to forgive it. For the situation did not arise. Three days later she heard from Rosa at the hotel's reception desk that Melford and the ladies Berger had checked out that morning on their return to America by non-stop jet.

'Throw big party last night. For 'm birthday, the Mister's, dey say,' Rosa reported with relish. 'Chef make 'm big cake on towers—' her flattened hand demonstrated the tiers of a ceremonial cake— 'ask plenty hotel guests. Missus le Conte, she there. Not Mister Vance. Not you, Missus Donna. But dey ask you for sure—yes?'

Donna replied truthfully that she hadn't known about the party, and not so truthfully that she couldn't have accepted if invited. So that was that, she thought. Incident closed. And in this, she conceded, Elyot had been right. She had been no more than a fill-gap for Melford Drinan after all.

Naturally she couldn't escape Bran's comments on Melford's pursuit of her and his sudden defection.

'Why all the enthusiasm for you, only to stand you up?' Bran wanted to know. 'Or did you stand *him* up before or after he imported a fiancée ready made? Down at the hotel they'd all decided it was a case, when surprise, surprise! he's off and you're not telling. So what did happen to break it up, for goodness' sake?'

'Nothing in particular.' Donna was grateful that no one who mattered, except Elyot, had witnessed or questioned Melford's blatant snub. 'It just wasn't a case in the way you mean—ever,' she added.

'Meaning you weren't ever turned on about him?'

'Meaning just that. Nor was he about me.'

'Well, obviously, since he had this other wench in tow all the while,' Bran agreed. 'Anyway, I'll believe you that you don't care. But you could have fooled *me*.'

It was a day or two later that Donna had a letter from her father asking if she had now learned enough about conditions at Louvet to feel she could sound Wilmot as to its future.

'We can't afford much longer for it to be as unproductive as it is at present,' he wrote. 'So as you say you know Elyot Vance of Marquise is interested in it, perhaps you're in a position to find out what terms he has in mind, and then from your uncle whether he would do a deal? Of course the Company would not care to ride roughshod over him, but if neither he nor Brandon are prepared to keep it up, we might have to go over his head in disposing of it.

'So I'm trusting you, dear, to approach both sides with tact and see what emerges. Meanwhile, make the most of your time to enjoy Laraye, as I know you will.'

Donna put aside the letter with a grimace. Easier said than done! One side—Elyot's— she couldn't now approach at all, with or without tact, and she doubted how far the same quality would go with Wilmot. Of course the Company would have to deal with both parties formally, but she understood her father's need to test the atmosphere first, so she supposed she must try. She decided to ask Bran to approach Elyot, and she tackled Wilmot herself.

As she had feared, her first exploratory questions brought his reaction that she had been put up to them by Elyot's coveting of the estate. This she was glad to be able to deny with truth, but she had to admit to her father's interest in the answers.

'Then you can tell him that he'd be better employed telling me how to conjure labour out of thin air and how to grow a commercially viable crop on soil as poor as Louvet's,' snapped Wilmot.

'But it's so close to Marquise. Is it possible for its soil to be very different and poor? Besides, if it's as poor as all that, would Mr Vance see any potential value in taking it into Marquise?'

That was a mistake, and Wilmot pounced on it.

'So now we have it!' he triumphed. 'If, as you say, you aren't in league with the fellow, how do you know he's after it?'

Donna did her best to recoup ground. 'I've neither seen him nor spoken to him about Louvet,' she said. 'But you know he would like to buy it, don't you, and I think it was Bran who told me so, soon after I came. And as Bran is quite frank that he isn't interested in Louvet, and you regard it as a burden in its present condition, I'd have thought—'

'Oh, you would, would you? Well, let me tell you this, young woman. While Elyot Vance is in the market for Louvet, and could outbid anyone else for it, no doubt, I'm no party to its being put up for sale, and so you can tell brother George when you write whatever report you may have promised him—'

It was at this point of deadlock that Madame Hué descended—literally, since her car hurtled down the lane at breakneck speed—upon the interview, and being Madame Hué, she had no compunction in listening in and taking sides.

'The Greeks had a word for the likes of you, Wilmot,' she admonished him. 'Needn't remind you what it is, need I? Don't want Louvet yourself; bare your teeth at anyone else who'd relieve you of it; won't do what you could do better than any man—write a book—with illustrations—that all tourists would flock to buy. Bah, Wilmot Torrence, you haven't got the sense you were born with, man! But I, Irma Hué, your friend, know just what you are lacking. Shall I tell you what it is, hm?'

Wilmot's teeth could be heard to grind. 'Not until I've told you, Irma Hué, to keep your nose out of my affairs,' he growled.

Her fat shoulders shrugged. 'Is that all that is new? Why, you tell me the same thing every time we meet, my friend. And so, for your lack of originality, I shall *not* now tell you what I know you need.' She turned to Donna. 'Run, child, and fetch the covered basket from my car. On the seat, yes. It is mangoes from Mousquetaire. You haven't a tree here, I know. We will take them together to Juno. Come.'

On the way to the kitchen quarters she suddenly chuckled. 'But you know what I threaten your bear of an uncle with, don't you, child?'

Donna thought back to their first meeting and smiled. 'Perhaps I can guess. A—wife?' she ventured.

'But of course, a wife. He has been without one for too long.'

'And have you anyone in mind?'

Madame Hué's eyes widened. 'Naturally,'

she said. 'Myself.'

★   ★   ★

In the kitchen they found Juno in an unusually sombre mood. Her smile did not flash and her tongue did not prattle, and in answer to Madame Hué's brisk questions as to what was wrong, she admitted she was 'troubled'.

'Troubled!' echoed Madame Hué. 'You are not ill; you have a good master and a secure place and no wild children to worry about. Nor, you should be thankful, a bad husband. So what ails you?'

Juno shook a head on which even the ribbon top-knot was limp. 'You say so, mistress, and all true. But it is not for myself that I worry. For my cousin Maria and her man Choc at Marquise, it is.'

'And what ails *them*, then?'

'Dey tink dey lose dere places, Mister Vance's cook and man.'

'Nonsense,' scoffed Madame Hué. 'Maria and Choc Baptiste belong to Marquise as a banana does inside its skin. Elyot Vance would be a fool to get rid of them, and Elyot Vance is no fool.'

'A good man too,' Juno confirmed.

'So why should this good man dismiss them? Has he told them they are to go?'

'Not yet he say to dem go.'

'Then why should they think he means to?'

But Juno either did not know or was not to be drawn as to the reason for their fears. She stated again, 'Dey tink so', and, further pressed by Madame Hué, added, 'Dey hear so' and 'People, dey talk, tell dem', but beyond that she would not go.

Madame Hué collected her basket from which Juno had emptied the mangoes, advised astringently, 'Tell them they make volcano out of anthill, and not to heed people's talk,' and then made a royal command of inviting Donna to luncheon at Mousquetaire.

As Donna feared it might be, the drive was a skin-prickling experience. At one point Madame Hué drove the nearside wheels of her car into a foot-deep rut at the road verge, whereupon she made a loud-hailer of her cupped hands, hollaed through them, summoning from an apparently empty landscape four or five youths who shouldered the car free, were rewarded with smiles and money, and melted again into their background as surprisingly as they had appeared out of it.

'When a woman finds herself in trouble, a man always comes along,' commented Madame Hué comfortably as she was enabled to drive on towards the next hazard, whatever it might be.

Mousquetaire perched on its steep hillside as if it had been flung there and had stuck. Donna never ceased to marvel at the narrowness of mountain shelves which had been judged wide enough to accommodate Larayan houses, and Mousquetaire was no exception. It jutted out above its precipitous approach like a beetling cliff.

For luncheon there was flying fish and a chicken-and-rice dish. With it Donna drank cool coconut water—a novelty to her— poured from a green coconut, hacked in two with a cutlass by Madame Hué's garden man.

Afterwards, as they sat on her verandah, she asked suddenly, 'You think me mad to suppose I could marry Wilmot, I expect?'

'Well—' Donna sought for a tactful answer, 'somehow I'd never visualised his rousing himself enough to marry again. He's so—so negative about anything outside his own interests.'

'Which is why a positive person like myself must take him in hand. I agree—he would not *marry*; therefore he must *be married*—find himself so, and I am working on it. You will see!'

Donna, remembering Wilmot's scathing criticisms of her hostess, doubted whether any amount of the latter's 'working' would bring him to the altar. But she was spared any comment as Madame Hué went on, 'Not that even I would take him on while he is so pigheaded over Louvet. *No* woman in her senses would marry herself to a brokenbacked banana patch by choice, and as I have all my senses about me, I think, he must sell it to Elyot Vance before I even consider giving him my Yes.'

Which, if it were true, gave Wilmot some breathing space, Donna thought with relief. For if Madame Hué were not going to lay concentrated siege to Wilmot's affections until he had sold Louvet to Elyot, she was likely to have to wait a very long time! And even her subsequent musing, 'Though who knows?—one may find ways, perhaps, of working on that too,' did not unduly disturb Donna for Wilmot's sake. On that score she could not see Irma Hué's power to budge him an inch.

At about four o'clock they set out on the return journey to Louvet. But nearing it by a few miles, Donna was puzzled at the road her

165

companion was taking, and said so.

Madame Hué nodded. 'That's right. I am not going straight to Louvet. We are making a detour first—to Marquise. If he is at home I am going to ask Elyot Vance the truth of these fears of the Baptistes, and if he is not, I shall find out from them.'

'But ought you to expect that you'll be told?' Donna asked, aghast, not only at her companion's interference, but that she herself was being carried uninvited to Elyot's home.

'I mean to be told. For how can one help, if one doesn't know what the trouble is?' Irma sounded satisfied with the sweet reason of her reply. 'And didn't I tell you that I am known for solving other people's problems—so long as they confide in me what they are—which, sooner or later, they usually do?'

To Donna's relief Elyot was not at home when they arrived. But when Choc answered the door to tell them so, Donna was shepherded ahead of Irma to the kitchen quarters, where Maria was dispiritedly chopping peppers for a salad.

'And now what's all this about your having to leave Mister Vance?' Irma demanded of her.

Maria's eyes widened. 'How you hear,

Missus Hué?'

'From your cousin Juno at Louvet. Who else? And so?'

Maria hung her head. 'Not right to say,' she said woodenly.

'Tcha!' Irma turned to Choc. 'You then—you tell me. What is it all about?'

'Well, Missus'—he hesitated, then plunged without his wife's permission—'Like this, see. Missus le Conte, she come up Marquise; say Maria not do things right; tell me *I* not do things right; grumble, find fault. Say she tell Mister we no-goods, and she make big change; send us away, get fine valet-man for Mister, and proper chef.'

Irma Hué nodded. 'Margot le Conte, eh? And when does she say you are to go?'

Choc shrugged. 'Dunno. Just say.'

Irma turned to Donna. 'She means when she marries Elyot, no doubt. Interesting, that. One hadn't heard he had decided on double harness just yet.' Of Choc she asked, 'Does Miss le Conte tell you this when Mr Vance is there? Did he tell her to say you must leave?'

Again Choc said, 'Dunno. But she not say it for sure, 'less he 'gree?'

'We'll see about that,' Irma ruled crisply. 'When do you expect Mr Vance to be in?'

167

But her question was not answered when there was a shout for Choc from the front of the house, and he leaped to obey it, followed through from the kitchen by Madame Hué and, reluctantly behind her, by Donna.

'Ah, Irma Hué. I saw your car.' Elyot took her hand. Without being told, Choc picked up a drinks tray and carried it off, and Elyot's glance went beyond Irma to Donna. 'Donna too. How are you?' he asked.

It was not a question to answer literally, and Donna hated herself for blushing at the memory of the last parting. Irma was saying, 'Donna has been lunching with me and I am taking her home to Louvet. No, we aren't staying for drinks. I only looked in to learn the truth of a monstrous thing we heard of first from Wilmot Torrence's Juno about your Choc and your Maria—that, at Margot le Conte's say-so, you are sending them packing. *Is* that so? Are you?'

Watching Elyot's inscrutable expression, Donna wondered how Madame Hué could possibly have expected that his loyalty to Margot would allow him to give a straight answer to the impertinence of the question. Nor did he. He said smoothly, 'You heard this from Juno, you say?' addressing Donna rather than Madame Hué, who cut in.

'*She* didn't. We did—just this morning, and only the smallest hint from Juno. But I've coaxed the details out of Choc, and now, Elyot Vance, I mean to hear from you whether or not it is true.'

'Why?' he asked.

It was the first time Donna had seen Irma nonplussed. 'Why?' she echoed. 'Well—'

'Would you perhaps be thinking of taking them on yourself?' Elyot pressed.

'No, of course not. I have my Winston and my Sadie—'

'Or could you, I wonder, have persuaded yourself that it's any of your business?' Elyot went on, as if she hadn't spoken.

'But of course it's my business!' she snapped back. 'As it would be the business of any of your friends who saw you making a fool and a knave of yourself at the behest of a woman! Don't forget, young Elyot, I first knew you when you were knee-high to a footstool, and over six feet tall though you may be now and cocksure with it, when I give you advice for your own good, you will kindly listen to it.'

He nodded. 'Willingly. *When* I've asked you for it in the first place.'

The sound which issued from Irma's lips was a small explosion. 'Come, Donna!' she ordered, stalking away. 'Doing a kindness; saving a man from his own folly—and what thanks does one get for one's trouble? None—none at all!'

Elyot, making no attempt to stop her, followed her out abreast with Donna, to whom, to her surprise, he said, 'Haven't we a provisional date for you to spend a shipment day on the estate? What about the next one—Thursday of next week?'

An olive branch? Or a sign of how trivially he remembered the acrimony in which their last meeting had ended; of how little a difference with her mattered to him? Donna heard herself saying, 'Thank you. I'd like that—if you can spare the time for me,' only to feel rebuffed by his careless, 'Good. I'll tell Couseau that you want to see the whole thing through, and he'll look after you. Do you want him to send a car for you?'

'No, I can walk over. It's no distance.'

'It means a very early start—soon after first light.'

'That's all right. I wake early.'

'And go prepared for any weather. If the heavens fall the shipment has to get away.'

'I'll do that.' His use of the word 'go' emphasised for her that he was consigning her to the care of his estate manager; that he wouldn't be there himself.

Madame Hué's parting shot to him, delivered from her driving seat, was, 'If you part from good faithful people like the Baptistes you will regret it, Elyot Vance!' To which he replied, 'You think so?' and waved the car away.

Presently, after some minutes of wordless huffing and puffing, she said to Donna, 'Of course what I really meant was that he's a fool if he allows Margot le Conte to wear the trousers for him already. Do you suppose he understood that?' And then, without waiting for Donna's reply, added, 'And what was all that about a date with you?'

'It was just that, as I haven't seen a consignment harvested or shipped from Louvet, he once suggested I should spend a whole shipment day on Marquise, and so suggested next Thursday.'

'You have been in touch with him then, since you met him by chance on your first day?'

'From time to time. He has been very kind.'

'And what does Wilmot say to that?'

'Mr Vance doesn't come to the house, but Uncle Wilmot knows I have seen him sometimes, and doesn't mind.'

'Which is more than you can expect of Margot le Conte, if she suspects Elyot of being too kind to a pretty girl like you. But that is no bad thing either—some corrective jealousy for that young woman who has always been too sure of her men by half.' Madame Hué nodded sagely. 'Yes, I for one would not be desolated for Margot le Conte to learn the hard lesson that a man like Elyot is only as faithful as his lack of opportunities allows.'

Donna said drily, 'Well, she also has been kindness itself to me and must know she could have no possible cause for jealousy of me over Elyot.'

'Then you would still claim, as you did at our first meeting, that you are not, as you would say, turned on by him, or as I would say, *bouleversée*, bowled over? Extraordinary!' marvelled Madame Hué.

'Why should it be?' Donna hedged.

'Because—' Madame Hué actually slowed the car for the plunge into the house lane— 'because if he weren't the high-handed, self-satisfied tycoon that he is and just about as pigheaded as Wilmot Torrence, which makes two of them, I might fall for him myself,' she concluded as she rocketed down the lane and brought the car to a standstill within a yard of the cliff-guarding crotons for the second time that day.

CHAPTER SEVEN

When Donna had told Madame Hué that Margot had been kind to her, she had been entirely sincere. Though they had little in common and a very little of the other girl's extravagant company was more than enough for her, she supposed that Margot probably tolerated her to about the same degree. So that Bran's blunt question of the following day found her totally unprepared for it.

'And what have you been up to, to get so thoroughly on the wrong side of Margot?' Bran wanted to know.

'I? On her wrong side? So far as I'm aware, I've done nothing to upset her. What do you mean?' Donna frowned.

'Well, having just gathered that you're by no means one of her favourite people, I wondered why,' said Bran.

'You gathered? How? What has she said to you about me, then?'

'About you, but not to me. I happened to be listening in uninvited.'

'Oh, Bran—eavesdropping?'

'Why not, when I realised she was talking about your Melford Drinan fiasco?' Bran paused. 'You do seem to have let her make a fool of you over him, don't you, my pet?'

'I don't know what you're talking about,' Donna sighed. 'For goodness' sake, begin at the beginning and explain.'

'Well, it was at her last night's weekly cocktail party. Margot was gossiping with her dearest rival, the manager's wife from L'Hotel Atlantique on Bayonet Bay. I was standing solo nearby. The two of them were swopping boasts about the Top People they'd landed this season; the Court Circular and New York's Four Hundred had nothing on the list of the names they dropped. And when Margot quoted Melford Drinan of Hexagon Inc. and Mrs Tours came back at her with an oil-sheik plus bodyguard, Margot switched the interest back to Drinan by saying next, "The joke was that while he was here alone, before his fiancée and her mother—they're Bergers, you know—came down to join him, he took a temporary fling with one of my little girl tourist guides, a young innocent without a *clue*, my dear. Flattered to her eyebrows, of course, but dropped flat when the Bergers arrived and the Berger girl retook

174

possession." Or words to that effect,' Bran concluded.

Donna felt suddenly cold, but tried to brace herself. 'And by the "little girl", Margot meant me, you knew?'

'Who else?'

'Of course. So what did Mrs Tours say then?'

'She sounded sorry for you. She said, "Poor child! But if she was as green as all that, shouldn't someone have warned her not to get involved?" And then, as if she'd been sharpening her knives in readiness for Margot, she went on very sweetly, "You, dear, for instance? Do you mean to say *you* didn't know all about Melford Drinan's having a Berger daughter for a fiancée before any of them came down to Laraye?" Which—as no doubt the Tours woman intended—rather put Margot on the spot, didn't it?'

'How did it?' asked Donna dully.

'Well, either she had to admit that she wasn't all that well informed, or that she could have warned you and hadn't. Anyway, she threw you to the lions by snapping back, "But of course I knew. What are gossip columns for?" Not being willing to have it supposed that she wasn't entirely *au fait* with all the details of her clients' social life, you see, she preferred to take any blame that was coming to her for not putting you wise when she could have done.'

'And did she really know Melford was engaged, do you think?'

'Sure thing, I'd say. Trust Margot,' said Bran with conviction.

'So did Mrs Tours hand out any blame?'

'Mildly. She murmured something about, In her place, she'd have thought it only fair to put you on your guard, etc, etc ... But Margot only shrugged and said, "Who would suppose nowadays that any girl out of her teens couldn't recognise and avoid a wolf—if she wanted to?" And then something about, So whose fault was it, if you took a tumble when he let you down? Which, when she switched the talk to something else, left me with the distinct impression that she might have been gunning for you for quite some time, and I asked myself why then, and now I'm asking you,' Bran finished, slightly out of breath.

Angry and bewildered, Donna couldn't tell him. 'Did you do anything? Say anything? Intervene?' she asked.

'How could I? It wasn't as if she had slandered you or lied about you. She'd only shown herself to be supremely mean.'

'Though she did lie about me without knowing it. For as I told you at the time, I didn't take any tumble over Melford Drinan. We were never on the terms she concluded we were. But it does show I've been wrong in thinking she liked me—well, moderately at least, whereas now it seems she hasn't had any use for me ever since—'

As Donna paused, searching her memory, Bran prompted, 'Ever since when?'

But she couldn't name a precise point in time. All she knew was that if Bran were right about Margot's pre-knowledge of Melford's engagement, she must somehow have earned Margot's enmity before that afternoon when Margot had congratulated her so expansively on her capture of his interest and had enthused in the same vein over the telephone to Elyot.

So early then in their relationship? Donna questioned. But since when or why, she had no idea, and told Bran so, convincing him, she thought.

When she was alone she wondered whether she could expect Bran to challenge Margot on her behalf, though she realised she couldn't. To do so would be to admit his eavesdropping, for which Margot was likely to give him short shrift. Besides, he enjoyed his work for her too much to risk her displeasure merely in defence of a cousin. But if Margot represented a rewarding meal-ticket for Bran, Donna had no such need to placate her, nor to oblige her any longer as a 'little tourist guide', and Donna couldn't wait to opt out as soon as she had fulfilled her current appointments. She did so by asking Rosa to take no more bookings for her, and she notified Margot in a guarded letter, thanking her for asking her co-operation and affording her the chance to explore the island, but claiming that now, possibly within weeks of her return to England, she ought to give more time to Louvet and her uncle's interests, hoping that Margot would understand.

In the circumstances she didn't really expect Margot's complacence, and she wasn't going to get it, as Margot, having sent no reply in writing, made clear as Donna was leaving the hotel after her last assignment.

Margot waylaid her and asked her into her office, where with her usual over-emphasis of the most ordinary remarks, she declaimed tragically, 'Darling, this is so *sudden*! You can't mean to do it to me—you really can't!'

Donna cringed from the falsity of

'Darling'. How completely insincere was it possible to get? 'I must, I'm afraid,' she said shortly.

'But why, my pet, *why*? At the very height of my season and you such a total success with everyone you took out—why?'

(If you don't know why, you'd better start guessing.) Aloud Donna said, 'I told you my reasons in my letter. I came to see my uncle and Bran and Louvet and to discuss some problems on my father's behalf, and we've made very little headway yet. I've got to give them more time than I have up to now.'

'Pff! As if we didn't all know Louvet is past hope, darling. And, hand on heart, *would* you say Wilmot Torrence either notices or cares whether you're there or not?' Margot coaxed, but after Donna had doggedly said nothing, her tone changed, turned ugly.

'I *see*,' she nodded. 'It suited you to make a convenience of my offer to give you a free run of the island, a lot of free meals, social openings, but as soon as it suits you better not to honour your side of the bargain, you decide to skip—isn't that so?'

Donna allowed fairly, 'It could look like that to you, but I did give you notice in writing and I told the desk not to book any more tours for me.'

'For reasons which a blind man could see through!' Margot scoffed. 'Oh no, my dear. I know perfectly well why you are piqued enough to let me down. You were so flattered by Melford Drinan's attentions and you set such store on snaring him that when his fiancée turned up and you realised he had just been playing around, you felt you had to blame someone, and you've picked on *me!* This was the only way you could think of getting back at me, and so—'

Donna said evenly, 'All I've done is to end an arrangement which suited us both when we made it, and I think I've honoured it as far as I was obliged to.' Looking Margot straight in the eye, she held her glance as she added, 'And how could I, in all justice, blame you, when you couldn't have known any more than I did that Melford Drinan was only marking time with me? Because if you had known, you wouldn't have encouraged me to cultivate him, would you? Even as a casual friend, you would have warned me against taking him seriously? Surely—wouldn't you?'

Margot bit her lip and looked away. 'Of course,' she snapped. 'What do you think?'

'That if you didn't, I couldn't possibly blame you, and don't,' said Donna. 'But equally I'm asking you to accept my reasons for not helping you any more, though at the same time thanking you for giving me the chance.'

'Oh, cut the formalities! You sound like a model letter of resignation from Every Businesswoman's Primer!' Margot declared. 'And meanwhile, since I *don't* accept your reasons at their face value, you will forgive me, won't you, if I make a shrewd guess that, since the job only produced for you a woman-chaser as a lover, you feel that, given the time for the hunt, you could do better on your own? Now let's see—what men have we introduced you to? Whom could you have in your range? Even Elyot for one, I shouldn't wonder. For another—'

'If that's your guess, I've no choice but to forgive you for making it, have I?' Donna cut in.

'No—have you?'

'Even though it's wrong.'

'Ah, but is it wrong?'

'Yes,' said Donna flatly, and turned on her heel.

Now she had made an open enemy, and it did not occur to her until later that she had probably allowed Margot to believe she had been deeply hurt by Melford's defection. She thought she had convinced both Elyot and Bran otherwise, but for the want of a firm word to the contrary, she had given Margot the petty triumph of thinking she had been painfully jilted. Later too Bran accused her of making too much of Margot's inexplicable hostility. He himself hadn't many illusions about Margot, but since Donna had enjoyed her tourist guide work, wasn't she doing the proverbial cutting off her own nose by opting out of it? To which Donna said 'Probably', but that her nose would be less injured than would her self-respect if she continued under any obligation to Margot.

Now her time was her own again, and contrastingly empty. She swam and sunbathed and walked alone, and when Bran was not using the mini-moke she mastered it sufficiently to drive it into the town to do shopping for the house. It was while she was down there on the afternoon before she was due to spend the day on Marquise that she was hailed across Navarre Street by Irma Hué in her car, stopped so abruptly that it rocked on its ancient springs and evoked hoots and angry yells from the frustrated drivers behind it.

Unperturbed, Irma waved them through and repeated her call to Donna. 'Hé, Donna

182

child—something to show you! Come over, will you?'

Donna, who had parked the mini-moke and was walking, went across. 'Get in,' Irma ordered and, as casually as if she and her car had a deserted racetrack to themselves, went on, 'What do you think? After being so rude, as good as ordering me out of his house, Elyot Vance—'

'Yes, well—' Donna cut in, in favour of the increasing stream of traffic the car was holding up, 'oughtn't you to move on, find somewhere to park? You aren't very popular, stopping here, you know. People sound as if they're getting mad.'

'M'm, so they do. Can't wait a moment nowadays, folks.' Glowering at the first car she waved on, Irma went into gear and shot forward herself, grazing a kerb as she turned abruptly on to St Vincent Square where she found a parking slot under the saman trees and halted the car again.

'Now,' she turned to Donna, 'about Elyot. Just as if we had last parted with kisses, he rang me up the other day—something he wanted me to do for him; something he thought that only I could do.'

'And you said?' Donna prompted.

'Forgave him, of course, as one does with

men like Elyot, and asked what it was, though he didn't tell me until he had asked whether I remembered the appearance of the Dial House before your uncle let it go to ruin, and even further back than that, to the time when the whole area was under sugar and the estate planter had lived there. To which I said of course I did, but why did he want to know.'

'So why did he?'

'Because he wanted me to do a painting of it—in watercolour or oils, as I pleased—to give his architect the idea of how he wanted it restored, exactly as it was, say, up to twenty years ago, before sugar failed entirely, and when Marquise and the rest of the area were not fully on bananas. About when it was singing its swan-song, he said, before it was left to stand empty for years.'

'I remember it faintly myself from about twelve or fourteen years ago,' said Donna. 'It was painted bright red all over, picked out in green, and there really was a sundial in the courtyard.'

'And so I've shown it—look!' Irma produced a portfolio from which she drew an unmounted painting in watercolours. 'He can have it in oils instead if he wishes,' she said. 'But I'm taking this up to him to see if it meets his idea of what he wanted. Does it meet your memory of it, child—tell me?'

Donna was prepared to be pleased, and was. The walls of Mousquetaire were hung with tasteful paintings of flowers, still life studies and landscapes, all proving Wilmot's scorn of Irma's skill as an artist to be yet another of his sour prejudices. And the Dial House, as Donna's childhood memory pictured it, had come to life under her brush.

Irma's angle of view of it was just right. Its reds were gaudy, its greens were vivid; the tub flowers which be-decked its balcony a flamboyant mass of colour, its surrounding paved courtyard and its sundial a sombre grey by contrast. Donna breathed, 'It's *just* like! Exactly as I think I remember it!'

Irma shared her appraisal of the painting. 'You think Elyot will approve it for his architect?'

'I'm sure he should. But—' Misgivings had struck Donna.

'But what? You have doubts, child?'

'Well, it's my uncle's property. Is he likely to give Elyot the right to restore it as he wishes?'

'Huh! Who pays the piper—'

Donna took that as a literal question and answered it. 'The Company will,' she said.

'Tch! Such ignorance of your own proverbs! It's to be Elyot's time and Elyot's men, and Elyot's right to call the tune of how it's to be done, isn't it? Not your Company's, all the way from England, and certainly not Wilmot's, who could have rebuilt the place as Noah's Ark or the Taj Mahal, *if* he hadn't preferred to watch it fall apart about his ears,' ruled Irma tautly. She put away the painting and made ready to move off. Donna got out and waved her away, not relishing at all Wilmot's reaction to Elyot's latest move to override him. But she was pleased. If Elyot had his way—and she backed him to, though wondering what whim had prompted his plan for an exact restoration—she was going to like the thought, when she went back to England, of the Dial House a ruin no longer and of its sundial telling the hours.

★   ★   ★

She woke the next morning to a tropical downpour, the Devil's heavy curtain of cloud showing no break anywhere.

'What happens when it's as wet as this?' she asked of the sleepy Juno who had called her at first light. 'Do the men start cutting the crop, or do they wait until it clears a bit first?'

'Oh, dey cut,' yawned Juno. 'Banana ship sail midnight latest, wait for no man. Crop cut, carried, sorted for trash, washed, graded, packed, loaded, down on quay by eight evening—or else. But no need you go over Marquise yet, Missus Donna, do you drown on way.'

So Donna waited until the storm abated somewhat, when she set out clad in her own good raincoat, overshoes contributed by Juno and sheltered by the huge carriage umbrella which was the common property of the house.

She carried a picnic lunch in a deep pocket and with no wind to drive the rain either into her face or against her back, she rather enjoyed the walk over to Marquise, and by the time she reached the big main store and packing-station, the rain was already giving over. And as evidence that the cutting had indeed begun to time at dawn, the first loads of sorting were already coming in from the plantations in open trucks running on narrow-gauge rails, which were the legacy to the banana industry from the sugar harvests it had superseded.

Watching the waiting sorters' concerted rush upon the trucks, Donna reflected

187

amusedly that the cliché for all this would be 'All was bustle and confusion.' But that it was an ordered confusion was proved by the speed with which the trucks were cleared, the huge stems stripped of their protective wrappings and the dexterity with which the women workers separated the bands of fruit and picked the spent florets from the tips of each single banana.

Next came the first washing under a conveyor-belt stream of running water, and the discard of bruised or spotted fruit. A second washing left a film of natural latex upon the surface of the water; a third cleared the skins of traces of pest-sprays, and then the expertise of long experience graded and packed the bananas into the cartons in which, softly nestled, they would travel under refrigeration to England.

The crop came in; went through its routine; the piles of cartons became of the area and height of average rooms before the transport lorries checked them out and away—the whole process one of swift precision in sharp contrast to the consequent welter of discarded polythene, trash of leaves, stems, damaged fruit, tyre-tracks and trodden mud which formed the store's inevitable underfoot approach.

Time passed; it was noon and the meal-break before Donna realised it. She was preparing to eat her sandwiches when Maurice Couseau, who had had little leisure to spare for her during the morning, insisted on taking her to lunch at his bungalow. This, as was Elyot's house, was perched high, with a full view of the rolling acreage of Marquise. Over the meal with his young wife the talk was of the day's crop, its unexpected heaviness and the battle for the time needed to get it all away to the deadline of eight o'clock at the docks.

'What happens if you can't make the deadline? Donna asked.

'It *must* be kept—by us to eight p.m., by the loading dockers to an hour before sailing time,' was the blunt reply. 'We can ask for an extension, but we can't be sure of getting it, and as bananas begin to ripen at once, any that are left behind would make for dead loss.'

'And have any ever to be left behind?'

Maurice Couseau met that with a short laugh. 'On Marquise, never without very good reason, and to my respected employer nothing much short of a major Act of God which struck his whole work force at one fell blow would be likely to constitute a "good reason'',' he said. At which Mrs Couseau protested, 'Oh, Maurice, that makes Elyot sound like a positive monster!'

'Monster? Not a bit of it. Just a man with a flair for gauging just what he can expect of people and usually getting it—that's all,' he defended Elyot stoutly.

When they drove downhill again he dropped Donna among the banana lines, for her to watch the hacking down of the bunches and their loading on the heads of the waiting girls who would carry them so to the trucks. Amid cries of encouragement and a lot of laughter Donna tried on one of the coltas—the hard fibre crowns which spread the weight of the load without the girls' having to put up a hand to balance it. Their carriage was superb, long custom making nothing of the weight, but when a stem was placed on Donna's colta, her knees buckled and after a few tottering steps she had to beg to be free of it.

Towards the end of the afternoon she rode back to the sorting shed on one of the trucks which, arrived there, had to take its place in a queue of at least a dozen others as yet unloaded. The activity inside the shed was frenzied and matters were not eased by its having begun to rain again. The great

190

wooden doors had to be slid to and the humidity behind them was intense. Trucks which had been emptied turned and squelched away through the mud for fresh loads, the raw material of the skilled work which went inexorably on—against the clock.

Just inside the door where the truck put Donna down Maurice Couseau stood with Elyot, who nodded a greeting to Donna and said 'Just a minute—', delaying her from moving away as he turned again to his manager. 'How many more?' he asked him.

A figure was named, and both men looked at their watches.

'Going to be tight,' said Elyot.

'Too tight for comfort. Any chance of an extension?'

'Doubtful. Anyway,' Elyot glanced out at the pounding rain, 'this should slow things up a bit on the lines, and if we can absorb this backlog of stuff, we could catch up and be ready for the rest that's to come in. Let's go.'

As the manager moved off Elyot turned again to Donna. 'This is Marquise with its shirt off—the tatty end of the business deal which finishes up on the ice-cream counters as banana split. What do you think of it?' he asked.

'I'm glad to have seen it. It's exciting. Is it

always as hectic as this?'

'Not always, though when it isn't, our pride needs to pretend that it is, it being a tradition in the local clubs that no planter worthy of the name ever admits to having suffered a light shipment day. It isn't done; honour must be served.'

Donna looked about her. 'Is there anything I could do to help?'

'Is there anything you think you could do?'

'I don't know. Perhaps—well, I might pick off the little flowers on the bananas.'

He shook his head. 'A bit of a puny contribution. Our girls have quicker fingers than yours. But something that would help— could you collect all these moppets who are hindering their mothers, and keep them quiet in a corner? Are you good with children?'

Donna looked about her at the toddlers who were underfoot, variously pulling at their mothers' skirts, fighting among themselves and playing improvised games with discarded bananas. 'I don't know,' she said. 'I'm very fond of them. But would they come to me?'

'If you do a Pied Piper act with the lure of some goodies that Couseau keeps in the office against emergencies like today's overtime working for the girls, who'd be taking their babes home about now on a less busy day. Then perhaps you could tell them a story or organise a game. Anyway, wait around, and I'll lay on the operation!'

The children came willingly enough, squatting round Donna, round-eyed and eager as she shared out the sugared biscuits and sweetmeats which Elyot brought to her before rolling up his sleeves and helping one of the team of men clamping shut and stencilling 'Marquise' on the cartons of fruit.

A game? Or a story? A round or two of Hunt the Banana proved popular; Oranges and Lemons, less so, since no one wanted to make an archway with Donna, thus missing out on the heady excitement of being caught under it. They played Tig until the younger ones tired, and then Donna, despairing of choosing a story acceptable to such mixed ages, hit on the idea of suggesting that they tell her a Larayan story instead.

She did not want for volunteers. Though the stories, charactered for the most part by over-proud cockerels, villain snakes and mild-mannered cows, were only a few sentences long, each was followed by a clamour of 'I tell now!'—'I tell 'bout—!' and the narrators had to wait their turn.

During the recital the apparent babe of the

party, a chubby brown ball with a curly black cap of hair, climbed on Donna's lap and went to sleep there, and she was still nursing him when she was aware of Elyot standing behind the group, watching and listening, not interrupting the stories. Her glance met his. He signalled a thumbs-up and smiled, then came across to her. 'Nursery session over,' he said. 'Thanks a lot.' He patted the sleeping boy's head, his touch gentle. 'The girls have finished, and we shan't be long. Would you like to deliver this one to his mother, or shall I?' he asked.

'I will.' The mother came to meet Donna, clucking her thanks and inviting Donna's admiration for her son's ability to sleep wherever he found himself. 'Dis one—he good boy, sleep proper in bed. But papa say, put him in coop wid chicken, peg him on line wid washing, he sleep jes' same,' she claimed as she tossed him up to her shoulder and bore him away.

Emptied of the chattering women, the big store quietened. Both the manager and Elyot had disappeared; men were loading the last of the cartons, and Donna stood alone, irresolute as to whether she ought to see Elyot before she left. Then the telephone rang in the office near which she was standing. No one was in there, and no one came to answer it. Donna let it ring for a time, then decided it had better be answered, as a call here was sure to be a business message which ought to be passed on.

She picked up the receiver. 'Marquise store office here. Yes?' she said.

There was a silence. Then Margot le Conte's voice came, sharply questioning. 'Who is that, then? Who is speaking?'

'Donna Torrence.'

Another silence. Then a smothered exclamation, 'What the—? What are you doing there? I'm calling Elyot. Choc said he was down there. So where is he?'

Donna said, 'I don't know for the moment. He's been here—'

'And left you in charge of his telephone—how cosy!'

'I've been watching a shipment at his invitation. The last of it is just about to leave, as I am myself. I was alone in the store when the telephone rang, and as nobody seemed to be going to answer it, I did. And I daresay I can find Mr Vance for you if you'll hang on,' Donna offered coldly.

'No, I can't wait. You can give him a message instead,' said Margot ungraciously. 'Tell him, will you, that Ella and George

195

Martin—have you got that, the Martins?—are going back to England by the banana ship tonight. I'm seeing them off, and I want him to join us in their cabin for drinks as soon as he can get here.'

'And where is "here"?' Donna asked.

'On board. We're waiting. He's coming down to see the shipment loaded, I daresay?'

Donna had wondered whether she might be asked to watch the loading, but if Margot was to be there, she felt nothing would persuade her to accept the invitation. She told Margot, 'I suppose he will.'

'Well, just give him my message, will you?' Margot replied without, Donna was thankful, the extravagant gloss of endearments which, from almost the beginning of their acquaintanceship, must have been false. The hostility which had been none of Donna's making was open on both sides now.

She was replacing the receiver as Elyot and his manager came back. 'I took a call for you as you weren't here,' she explained, and gave him the message as she had had it from Margot.

He nodded. 'Right. Thank you. Then let's go,' he said.

The three of them went out of the big main

doors, which Maurice Couseau locked behind them. It had stopped raining, but between them and the men's two cars there lay a quagmire-cum-lake of richly churned mud and water. Elyot looked at Donna. 'We can't ask you to ford that,' he said.

'I could. I borrowed some overshoes from Juno.'

'All the same—' An arm went across her shoulders, another behind her knees and before she could protest he was cradling her and squelching out across the morass, Couseau following. Setting her down beside his car, he tapped the glass of his watch and said to the other man, 'We shall have made it, after all.' Then he opened the passenger door for Donna, who shook her head and stood back.

'I'll walk home,' she said. 'It's a lovely evening after the rain. And thank you very much—' she shared a glance between both men—'it's been a fantastic day.'

Elyot stared, his expression hardening. 'You're seeing it through? You're coming to watch the loading?'

'No. I've seen that part before—from the dockside. I'll walk back now, if you don't mind.'

He compressed his lips. 'Very well.' He

took his own seat, said, 'Maurice, see Donna back to Louvet, will you? She isn't walking, after being on her feet since heaven knows what hour this morning. I'll go straight on down. See you there—' and drove away. Away to join Margot at Margot's imperious invitation, leaving Donna to guilt at having rejected him and with nothing for comfort but the memory of the smile he had sent her across the heads of the children and of the too-brief experience of his carrying her across the mud. The former had been no more than approval of her role as nursemaid; the latter merely a piece of male chivalry. But her imagination needed to see them both as his willing bridging of the rift between them. For they were all she had to set against her jealous mind-picture of him and Margot together, laughing, drinking, making love... All.

CHAPTER EIGHT

However exaggerated had been Margot's taunt that Wilmot scarcely noticed Donna's presence, he was certainly the last of anyone close to her to realise that she no longer had Melford Drinan's escort, nor kept any appointments at the Allamanda.

Even Juno had commented with a hearty, 'You stay home more now, Missus Donna. That good. F' one ting, feed better here wid Juno's cooking, and maybe make the Mister eat proper, you feed wid him.'

And Irma Hué had been quick to see Donna as a now leisured special pleader of her own cause with Wilmot. 'You spend more time together now. So—just a hint here and there that you are surprised he doesn't get rid of Louvet and feel free to do his own thing, as you young people would say. Or tell him perhaps how much you admire my work and how well you think he and I could collaborate on a book. Nothing too blatant, you understand, child? Just the odd word in his ear which should keep me in his mind,' she urged, happily blind to the fact that Wilmot's sales resistance to the mere mention of her name was absolute.

But though Wilmot's reaction was tardy, when it came it was unexpectedly compassionate. A propos of nothing, he said one morning, 'That fellow who used to call for you, take you out—you don't see him any more? Why not?'

Donna said, 'Melford Drinan? He was only on a business trip, as I think I told you,

Uncle. And he's gone back to America now.'

'"Gone back"—just like that? Amused himself, then took off—was that it?'

She shook her head. 'It wasn't like that. He already had a fiancée—'

'Was frank about having one? Told you so straight away?'

'No,' she admitted. 'In fact, I didn't know he was engaged, until his fiancée and her mother came down to Laraye, and they all went back together later.'

'Jilted you, eh?' Wilmot took a long draught of coffee and wiped his lips. 'Well, it happens,' he said.

'Yes—' Expecting that to be the sum total of his sympathy, Donna was about to assure him of how little but her pride had been hurt, when he went on to repeat,

'Yes, it happens. But when you're young and it does, it seems to split your world apart, eh?'

When the man you love doesn't want you, it *stays* apart, was Donna's swift thought, though not of Melford Drinan. Aloud she agreed, 'Yes, I suppose so.'

'And yet—' Wilmot paused. 'Well, if it's any help, there's a Larayan saying that you might do well to think of and remember. You wouldn't understand it in *patois*, but its gist
200

is, "One ship gone to the bottom won't prevent another's sailing." You understand how its meaning could relate to a broken love-affair. It makes its point?'

'Yes indeed.' Donna knew she ought to disillusion him as to how little she had been hurt at Melford Drinan's hands, but her thoughts were racing in another direction. She had never talked on any intimate level with Wilmot before, but it sounded as if he were trying to console her from his own experience, and if that meant he had realised at last the futility of enduring bitterness over the might-have-been, could she hope it had dispelled at least one cause for his hostility to Elyot?

In face of his own ineptitude, he might still resent Elyot's success, but if he had rid himself of the deeper canker of holding Elyot's mother's unfaithfulness against her son, wasn't that one step towards a tolerance which might make them, if never friends, something less than the open enemies they were now?

Donna said again, 'Yes,' and treading warily, added, 'Are you telling me, Uncle, that you yourself have found it to be true—that in time one gets over anything and is able to—to set sail again?'

He sighed. 'In time, yes. Though it can sometimes take a lot too long. You shouldn't let it rankle too long for you.'

'I won't,' she was able to promise frankly. 'In any case, my affair hadn't gone very far. But you're telling me that at some time there was someone for you whom you had to "get over", and that you did in the end?'

'When I was a young man, yes, and my affair had gone deep. But I married your aunt Winifred, didn't I? And it's she whom I've missed since she died. Not the—other one.'

Donna said warmly, 'I'm glad you were happy with Aunt Winifred, but thank you for telling me as much as you have.' It occurred to her that here Irma Hué would expect her to dash in with a suggestion that, having known contentment in one marriage, he might be prepared to consider another. But for Donna by far the more important issue was the possibility of the end of Wilmot's cold war against Elyot; Louvet, cultivated and fruitful once more; Wilmot himself with cause no longer for his sour frustration; Elyot's ambition for Marquise and Louvet fulfilled.

When she went back to England she would go heart-empty. But at least that was a picture she would be glad to remember she had left behind. None of it would be her doing, of course—simply a change of purpose and direction on Wilmot's part. And if he were already on the way to that—?

But that he was not, at least in the matter of the sale of Louvet to Elyot, was evident from his reception of her tentative suggestion of how much she would like to see Louvet in as full production, comparatively speaking, as Marquise.

'As conditions are, that's impossible,' he snapped.

'I know. For one thing, without Bran's help, you've had no choice but to neglect it,' she soothed. 'But isn't that an argument for getting rid of it while you can, before it deteriorates so far that nobody will buy it? And if you were prepared to sell it, you must know the Company would back your decision, surely?'

'Just so—expecting me to take the offer of the highest bidder!'

Though fearing what was coming next, Donna said, 'Well, naturally. That's business.'

'With which I'll have no part, while that fellow Vance is in a position to be able to outbid anyone else.'

Deadlock. Donna tried another tack. 'Bran

says,' she remarked, 'that your real ambition is to set up a reserve in the rain forests for all the native Larayan flowers and shrubs. Will you ever be able to do that?'

'No money to buy the land.'

'Who owns the land?'

'It's mostly Government owned, and it would require acres.' Wilmot paused, then, as if making the offer were an effort, added, 'If you're interested enough, I could drive you over the area I have in mind—down south, inland, where a lot of the soil would be virgin and ideal.'

'I'd like that,' Donna told him. And it was from that talk and his keeping of that promise that she was able to date a closer understanding with him, confirming her earlier guess that it was the commercialism of Louvet which irked him. He loved all nature for its own sake; trading in it was obnoxious—a principle which admittedly wouldn't have got humanity far on the way to civilisation, but which she supposed the few eccentrics like Wilmot must be allowed to indulge and live by, as far as they could.

At least Madame Hué claimed to take hope for her own plans from his airing of his ambition to Donna. Nodding thoughtfully as she worked it out, 'So that if he could get the land for his old reserve, he might be willing to let Louvet go,' she pondered.

'Not, I'm afraid, if it meant Elyot Vance could buy Louvet,' Donna warned.

'Bah, the stubborn old mule!' Madame Hué exclaimed disgustedly. 'Here you have one man with his hand in his pocket, ready to buy, and another who should have sense enough to sell something he doesn't value. But put them each side of a table to discuss a deal, and where are you? Why, exactly where you were before, my friend! And yet ... and yet,' thoughtfully again now, 'there must be ways. Yes, indeed there should be ways. One must just continue to work on it, that's all.'

Changing the subject, she reported that Elyot himself had had enough sense to listen to her plain words on the subject of Margot's threat of dismissal to Choc and Maria. When she had taken her painting of the Dial House up to Marquise, she had made it her business to question them, to hear—as Donna had already heard from Juno—that he had no plans at all for getting rid of them; that Miss le Conte had made a mistake in believing that he had.

Unfortunately for Donna's peace of mind, Juno's version had been slightly different. For Juno, reporting that Elyot had used a word she didn't know, but which meant Missus le Conte had been 'afore herself' or 'afore-hand' with her threats, offered Donna no comfort. If Elyot had said Margot had been 'premature', which was likely, then 'premature' was probably all Margot had been—jumping the gun of her future sway over Marquise when she was Elyot's wife, but already very sure of the rights she would demand of him and get, once she was.

Meanwhile, with no choice but to bow to the Company's ruling about the Dial House, Wilmot maintained his dignity by ignoring the fact that anything was going on there.

But something was. Donna too had indulged him by refraining from mentioning the place, but she did go down one day with Madame Hué, who, since Elyot's acceptance of her sketch, claimed a designer's right to see how her ideas were being carried out. And considering how little noted for speed Larayan artisans were, Donna was surprised by the progress the builders had made.

The walled courtyard had been repaved and a new sundial set up. Though it was still littered with builders' rubble, there were the makings of a garden; the rooms were clean and refloored; the broken stairs had been torn out and replaced, and the balcony of embarrassing memory for Donna was sturdy and brave in its new gaudy dress of red paint, in startling contrast to the bright emerald of the main entrance.

Madame Hué approved it. Elyot, she told Donna, had had to fight his architect to have it restored just so. The man had advised razing the house to the ground, rebuilding it one-storeyed and flat-roofed, the finish to be white overall. But Elyot had insisted that it be executed exactly to the sketch. '"For sentiment's sake", he told the architect,' Irma reported. 'Though what sentiment he could possibly feel for a house that he didn't own and wasn't on his land, I suppose he must have left the poor fellow to guess. But he got his way. As always.'

'Considering how everything in Laraye gets the treatment of the brightest colours anyone could dye or mix, Elyot probably meant for tradition's sake, not sentiment's,' Donna suggested. 'And as I told you when you showed me your sketch, I remember this place exactly as you had it. Except—' She paused, shading her eyes as she looked up at the end gable beneath which they were standing. Except that there was a clock up there in the wall, just under the eaves.'

'A clock? *I* don't remember any clock,'

Irma claimed.

'But there was. I remember—' Donna broke off and turned as Elyot's car stopped on the road and he got out and came over.

'Donna says there used to be a clock in this gable. But there wasn't. If there had been, I'd have remembered it,' Irma attacked him.

He looked at Donna. 'Clock—or no clock?' he inquired.

'Clock,' she affirmed with a nod.

'No clock,' Irma insisted. 'She was only a little girl when she left Laraye, and she must be mistaken. Besides,' she added with simple logic, 'if they had an outdoor clock, what did they want a sundial for?'

Elyot laughed. 'Probably so that each could shame the other into telling the right time. Irma, *ma mie*, don't be so innocently literal, for Pete's sake. And Donna would hardly have imagined a clock, would she?'

'She might have seen a clock on some other house-gable, and thought it was here.'

'Still, I think we'll let her have her clock,' he adjudicated. 'I'll arrange to have one installed.'

Irma shrugged. 'I thought you wanted the restoration to be exact. But you'd rather take Donna's version than mine?'

'Just in case Donna is right,' he said

208

quietly, causing Donna to wonder why he should choose to champion her in the petty argument, as if it mattered either way.

Fortunately Irma never remained ruffled for long, and when Elyot excused himself, saying he had to speak to his foreman, she stayed him.

'About our affair—are you expecting me at Marquise tonight?' she asked.

'So we arranged.' He paused. 'Does Donna know?'

'No.'

'Nor Brandon?'

'Yes. After I saw you yesterday, I rang him at the Allamanda and he promised to bring Donna along.'

Donna looked a query at both of them. 'What is all this about?'

Elyot said, 'Irma will tell you,' and left. And Irma, slightly on the defensive, said, 'Of course I was going to explain. It's a business matter I brought up with Elyot which indirectly involves you and your cousin, and Elyot suggested we all meet at Marquise to discuss it. Will you come?'

'If you think I should. But what kind of business?' Donna puzzled.

'I don't know that I ought to tell you before Brandon knows,' Irma evaded.

'I thought you said he did?'

'No, I only meant that I had asked him to come to meet Elyot tonight, and he's coming. So let's leave it until then, may we?'

Reluctantly, her curiosity aroused, Donna left it, and Bran, questioned, knew no more than she did. He borrowed his father's car, and all the way over to Marquise they canvassed each other's opinions as to what 'it' could be all about.

Irma was there before them. Elyot poured fruit punches and they settled on the verandah. 'Shall I explain, or will you?' Irma asked him, and did so in answer to his, 'It's your idea. Go ahead.'

'Well, it's about Louvet,' she began. 'We all know how things stand. Wilmot doesn't want it and won't work it. Elyot wants to add it to Marquise and make a success of it.' She looked at Donna. 'If it were put on the market for sale, your Company would expect Wilmot to take the offer of the highest bidder, and Elyot would see to it that his was the best offer. *But* Wilmot wouldn't sell to Elyot, he says. And so, as it's to the interest of all of you that it should be sold, I've suggested to Elyot that there is a way round that. Always supposing that we agree to take it, of course.'

There was a momentary silence. Then Bran said, 'I'd say I'm game for anything that would rid us of Louvet. But why should you bother?'

Irma flushed slightly. 'Because Wilmot is my friend, and he has been saddled with that white elephant for too long—'

'Which conjures up a most bizarre image—Dad buckling at the knees, while this milk-white elephant rides high. Wish I could draw,' murmured Bran. 'But go on—what's the scheme?'

'This,' said Irma. 'That somebody makes a private offer—of a size that it would be madness to refuse for Louvet in its present state—either through the Company or to Wilmot direct, and as it would come from quite a different quarter than from Elyot and would even appear to cut him out, mightn't Wilmot be fairly likely to take it?'

Again silence as Donna and Bran digested this. Then Donna repeated, '"Somebody"? Who?'

Irma shrugged. 'Just someone. It wouldn't matter who.'

Donna felt a chill of foreboding. 'A—a *fictitious* person, you mean? A cover for someone else who was really putting up the money? It would all be done under wraps—

through solicitors or something, until it was signed and settled? But all the time there wouldn't *be* this mythical purchaser.' She looked straight at Elyot, through him. 'The offer would really be—yours?'

He inclined his head. 'That was the idea.'

'And Irma's, you say? But you go along with it? You're willing to play? Just as Bran says he's game for anything to be rid of Louvet, so you're game for anything to get your hands on it? You'd even stoop to this—this charade of a scheme to deceive Uncle Wilmot, and I don't know how you dare!'

She broke off, her features working, as Bran put in, 'Easy, girl, easy! What's so wrong with it as a scheme, anyway? It would sell Louvet, which everyone agrees would be a good thing, and in doing it, it would save Dad's face, don't you see?'

'Save his face!' Donna echoed, almost beside herself. 'Save his face—for how long? For just so long and no longer, I suppose, than it suited you all to pretend that it wasn't Elyot who clinched the deal? So that when the time arrived for the cover to be dropped and for Elyot to start working Louvet, which would have to happen sooner or later, what about Uncle Wilmot's "saved" face then, you tell me? *What?*'

Her glance had travelled from one to the other of them, her outraged question addressed to them all, and each of them answered her in turn.

Irma said uncomfortably, 'But once Wilmot learned the truth, it would be too late, and he would have to come round in the end.'

Bran said, 'It sounds to me like a classic case of "ends and means". If the end result is satisfactory, what's wrong with the only means that are likely to bring it about?'

Elyot said, 'It doesn't seem to have occurred to you that we could have laid the thing on and carried it out without any obligation to consult you. Bran, yes, since he, as his father's son, has a financial interest in the future of Louvet. But you, no. It was simply that I, for one, wanted your reaction, and I'm sure Irma thought it fair to get it too.'

'And you've got it, haven't you?' she retorted furiously. 'Or must I spell it out that I think the whole thing is despicable and unworthy of any of you?'

'No, you've made yourself quite clear as to that already,' Elyot said evenly.

'Good,' she snapped, and looked at Irma. 'I *meant* I thought it was unworthy of you,' she said. 'I know you've interests of your own with regard to Uncle Wilmot and you want to see him rid of—how did you put it?—his broken-backed banana patch, but that you would hatch a plot like this and think I'd be a party to its going through—no? You say you're his friend, but who needs enemies with friends who can scheme like this?'

She dealt with Bran next. 'And you see nothing wrong with it? Just because it's a way of getting rid of Louvet, you'd stand by and see Uncle Wilmot tricked into the only way that could be achieved. Well, *I* won't. You'll all have to think again. And as for you—' she turned on Elyot, her voice shaking—'I suppose you are so used to getting your own way that it didn't occur to you you might fail this time if you backed Irma's scheme? Well, Bran warned me about you very early on— said that everything you touched was a success and there was nothing that power or money couldn't get for you. And it's money here, isn't it? *Secret* money. You've only to wave a big enough cheque, signed by any other name than yours, and you are home and dry—you hope.'

She broke off, needing to still her quivering lips. Still loving the shape, the presence, the potency of the man she'd thought he was, she hated the complacent duplicity which had fallen in with Irma's scheme; assuming that if money and deception would make it succeed, he'd go along with the deception, and the money—his—would be there to be used.

'You *hope*,' she repeated meaningly, and stood up, wiping off her damp palms, one against the other, as if ridding them of a taint. More controlled now, she added, 'Meanwhile, if any private offer for Louvet comes to Uncle, either through the Company or from anywhere else, I shall advise him to put it straight into the nearest rubbish bin, which is where it should belong. Is that clear?'

When no one answered her, she thrust aside the drink which she had scarcely touched, and moved far enough away to cause Elyot to rise and demand sharply, 'Where are you going?'

She turned. 'Home to Louvet,' she said.

'How?'

'If Bran isn't ready to come, I'll walk.'

'After dark? That distance? You'll do nothing of the kind. Brandon—!'

Bran didn't move. 'She's had her say, calling us all twisters. She can darn well wait until I'm ready,' he said sulkily.

215

Elyot's eyes flashed anger. 'She's going now, and she's not walking back alone. You will take her, and if she refuses to get into your car, I'll put her in bodily myself.' His imperiously jerked head brought Bran to his feet. Finishing his drink, he nodded 'See you—' to Irma and Elyot and followed Donna out, muttering as he opened the car door for her, 'Nice matey trip back *this* is going to be!'

★   ★   ★

Bran's sarcasm had been right about the drive back to Louvet, and was equally so with regard to the relations between himself and Donna during the time which followed.

When they had to do so, they spoke with studied politeness. Otherwise they avoided each other as far as was possible, and though Juno worried that young Mister now spent too much time at 'dat hotel', neglecting Donna, Wilmot's detachment from the everyday scene appeared to notice nothing amiss.

Irma Hué rang up once when Donna was out and left a message with Juno, suggesting that as she had something of interest to tell Donna, Donna should ring back. But Donna

216

did not ring; nor did Irma telephone again, and she did not come over. Elyot made no sign at all.

Thus isolated, Donna spent more time alone and increasingly more with her uncle. To her father she wrote that she saw no prospect ahead of his willingly quitting Louvet; that if the Company decided it must cut its losses, it must, in her opinion, act independently of Wilmot, and that, her trouble-shooting mission having failed, perhaps she ought now to return to England. If the estate were disposed of, she thought Bran could be trusted to be able to make his way in fields of his own choice, but she supposed and hoped that the Company would adequately pension Wilmot and perhaps allow him to retain the Louvet bungalow. She had not yet had a reply to this letter when Wilmot received a small bulky package by post from Elyot—the keys to the completed Dial House.

Wilmot showed them to Donna with a grudging 'Something, I suppose, for the fellow to acknowledge that it's my property he's been tinkering with. Want to go down and see what he's done with it?'

The suggestion surprised Donna, for on his own reluctant forays on to the neglected land, he must have seen the work in progress. But she went with him as willingly as she did now on any expedition he offered her.

The workmen had all gone, their rubble cleared; tubs of flowering plants were in place on the balcony, the floors were scrubbed, the windows were clean and there was a clock in the end gable. Wilmot tramped all over the building and the courtyard and said finally, 'It's as close to the original as I could have done it myself. But why should *he* bother, when his only concern was for his brats of trespassers? And how did he know what it looked like in the sugar days?'

Donna said, 'He must have remembered something about it; *I* could, and I think he asked Madame Hué to paint a picture of it as she remembered it, and his architect worked from that.'

'And how do *you* know all this?' Wilmot asked suspiciously.

'She showed me her painting before she took it to him,' Donna was able to answer with truth.

'Huh! Paint—Irma Hué? Wonder the architect was able to tell which way up to look at it,' Wilmot snorted.

'Well, I thought it was very good,' Donna felt obliged to admit.

218

'And what sort of judge of art are you?' he retorted tartly—a question to which he obviously expected no answer.

So the halcyon days of the dry season passed—cool blue mornings turning white with heat by noon, watered less often now by rain flurries which never lasted long, calm golden evenings when a clear sky paled to lemon, or a cloud-wracked one to purple and flame as the sun went down.

Anxious to learn the pattern of the climate and conditions in the months ahead when she would not be there—what about the torrid heat, the tropical rains, the risk of typhoons which the tourists shunned?—Donna heard from Juno the Larayan rhyme which said it all about the hurricane season—

'June—too soon;
'July—stand by;
'August—if it must;
'September—remember;
'October—all over,'

and though Juno assured her, 'Long time passing sin' hurricane catch Laraye. Cyclone no blow now'day,' Donna regretted that she would not know the heady, dangerous excitement of looking for a hurricane which might or might not come. Long before September or October she would have gone back to England.

Immediately ahead there loomed a day of Carnival for Calvigne. It would mark no particular event, no saint's day, no special reason for making public whoopee. But periodically the town needed both to let off its high spirits and to put on a show for the tourists, and for this purpose one day was as good as any other.

Donna heard of Carnival's promised delights from Juno and saw the preparations for it when she went down into the town. Bunting was looped between the lamp-standards; all the windows on the route of the carnival parade sported flags of every possible significance. Donna spotted among others the Red Ensign and the yellow cholera flag—Calvigne wasn't a cosmopolitan port for nothing! The shops and the market would be closed; the bars would be open. The schools, the town council, the Banana Growers' Association, the Yacht Club would be represented; five steel bands would accompany the parade; everyone's house-help and gardeners would expect the day off, or if not granted it, would take it. All the hotels were laying on parties and dances for the evening; the night-clubs expected to be serving breakfast the following day.

On the day itself Juno, peacock-garbed and flower-hatted, went down by bus to meet Maria and Choc. Bran offered Donna no invitation to go with him; he merely announced that he would be sleeping at the Allamanda that night. Wilmot said that one Larayan carnival was just like another and that in his lifetime he had already seen too many. Donna would probably like to see the parade, but she couldn't have the car as he would be needing it. So Donna, lacking both escort and transport, decided to go by the next bus to watch the morning's procession and displays, planning to get back before Wilmot did, probably in the afternoon. On leaving to catch the bus she asked when she could expect him and where he was going, and he told her, naming an area she knew in the rain forest. He would be back in time for dinner, well before dark, he said.

In the town the streets were a kaleidoscope of moving colour as a surging tide of Larayans, clad in their best and gaudiest, flowed over pavements and roadways, looking for the best vantage points from which to watch the parade. There was singing, there was laughter, there was picnicking on punches and hamburgers; the few cars which had ventured on to the streets

221

were jeered and catcalled as they came virtually to a standstill against the stream.

The very mass of humanity might have been frightening if it hadn't been so lighthearted and good-natured in expectation of a day which it meant to make its own.

Donna found a spot, shaded by a shop awning, from which to see the parade, which had begun at ten o'clock and was taking upward of two hours to snake and curvet and gambol its way round the town. The bands were spaced along its length, vying with each other to maintain a beat to which people could march; the banners of countless fellowships ballooned above the company; the decorated floats were the signal for screams of excited appreciation from the audience along the route. There were hideously masked devils and dragon men, children in space-gear, clowns, angels, cowboys. Every now and then things were held up while the clowns gave a tumbling act or the cowboys mimed a shoot-out against Red Indians. The ultimate goal of the parade was the town cricket-ground where a grandstand had been erected from which the floats would be judged.

Donna ordered a light lunch in one of the marquees on the ground, knowing she must exercise more than usual of the necessary patience in waiting to be served. She hadn't seen anyone she knew, but she didn't lack the companionship of people ready to chat and to invite her comments on the fairness or wicked prejudice shown by the judges. She stayed until the awards had been made, the parade disbanded and it was time to catch the return bus. She was glad to have seen Laraye at its gayest, most innocently jubilant. For all she had had to spend it alone, she was going to remember this day . . .

Back at the bungalow in the late afternoon, she had a swim, made herself a pot of lemon tea, collected the makings of a prawn vol-au-vent and fruit salad for dinner, then lay on a sun-lounger on the verandah, reading, until the sun went down.

Until then she hadn't expected Wilmot, and though he had promised 'well before dark', she didn't question his lateness until it was really dark. She busied herself laying the table, preparing the salad, mixing his pre-dinner punch and getting ready to put the vol-au-vent in the oven as soon as he came in.

But he did not come. Anxious now, more than an hour after sunset, she fidgeted from verandah to kitchen, making jobs to do, telling herself she mustn't worry. He had the car; it could have broken down where he could neither get help nor telephone. The road through from Soubion, his objective, was a lonely place after dark . . . too lonely, no more than a mountain track for part of the way. Donna shivered at the thought of Wilmot marooned somewhere up there, and though her reason argued that he must have been benighted by accident many times before, nothing of the sort had happened while she had been in Laraye, and she didn't know what to do.

At any other time Juno would have been there. So, about now, would Bran have been. But Juno, who would wait for the dancing and the bonfires, wouldn't be back for hours, and Bran had said he wouldn't be home that night at all. But something had to be done, someone must be told, someone who could help her, who had a car, as she hadn't one at her disposal.

She stood, hesitant, looking at the telephone. If she hadn't rejected Madame Hué's call to her, she might have rung Mousquetaire for advice. But Irma, anyway, was probably at the Carnival herself. It had to be Bran then. By now he was probably at the Allamanda for its evening party. Though supposing he weren't—?

She picked up the receiver, got the number, gave her message to the porter who answered, 'Mister Brandon? Dunno if he here, missus. But wait, I go find.'

He was a long time away. Donna fiddled with the telephone cord, picked at a stray thread on her dress, listened too for the sound of the car coming down the lane, and jumped in foolish dismay when a crackle in the receiver indicated that the porter had come back and was at the other end of the line. Or was it Bran?

'Yes? Yes?' she croaked impatiently. 'Is that you, Bran? Listen—'

But the voice which cut in upon her was neither Bran's nor the porter's. Of any voice she least expected to hear, it was Elyot's.

CHAPTER NINE

Elyot said, 'Donna? You wanted Brandon? Well he's been paged, but he doesn't seem to be here. Would you like to leave a message? He shall get it as soon as he turns up.'

She didn't know what to say. She had banked on being able to summon Bran and the mini-moke. 'Yes... no. That is—' she hesitated. 'Leaving a message won't do. Do you know perhaps where I could reach him?'

'Not a clue. He could be living it up anywhere in the town or at any other of the hotels. No message then to say what you want him for? Where are you ringing from, anyway?'

'From the bungalow, from Louvet. I'm alone here, and I need Bran to get back here—now.'

'Alone?' Elyot's echo was sharp. 'Where is Juno, then? And your uncle?'

'Juno is at the Carnival, and Uncle Wilmot drove down to Soubion, saying he would be back before dark. But he hasn't come, and I'm worried. Something must have happened to him, and that was why I was calling Bran. But if he isn't there—'

Considering the bitter tirade she had hurled at Elyot the last time they had met, she hadn't meant appeal to sound in her tone. But she couldn't keep it out, and when he responded to it she was ashamed.

'Soubion? That's all of thirty miles!' he exclaimed. 'Why there?'

'He's on one of his nature forays. I know the area he'd be making for—I've been there with him. There's a point where he leaves the car on the road—it's a terrible one—and walks up into the forest. And supposing he had had an accident, fallen perhaps, and couldn't get back to the car, or—' Now her defences were down and though she had thrown away the right to expect Elyot's willing help, she was openly begging that he wouldn't grudge it to her.

He didn't. He said, 'Right. Stay where you are. He may turn up yet, and you could be panicking without cause. But I'll leave straight away and drive up.' He rang off and she replaced her own receiver, looking at her watch then, wondering how she could fill the many slow minutes until he arrived. By now she didn't expect Uncle Wilmot to confound her fears for him. Her only lifeline to hope had to be Elyot.

He came in his estate car, which seemed to be loaded with an assortment of gear at the back—two powerful torches, an axe, a banana-worker's cutlass, a Thermos flask, a bottle of cognac, a first-aid kit, a blanket, pillows and a stretcher—all the latter, he explained, borrowed from the Red Cross post in the town which planned to be open for carnival casualties all night.

'A useful tool, a stretcher, when you can command four hands and you don't know what you're going to find,' he remarked, which afforded Donna the wry satisfaction that he took her fears seriously.

'You'll have to come with me to show where he's likely to be if he isn't held up on the road,' he told her.

'Of course.'

'Then get a warm coat and stout shoes; we may have to stay out and to climb.'

She joined him in the car after fetching the topcoat and lace-up shoes which had been comfortable autumn wear on her journey from England as far as Antigua, though not beyond. As he drove he put one or two questions as to times and Wilmot's habits of movement on his forays, and Donna broke the ensuing silence by apologising, 'It was good of you to come, when I couldn't contact Bran. I don't know what I should have done—called the police, I suppose.'

He shrugged. 'You would have preferred Brandon, naturally. But you should be glad it was only the shank of the evening as far as my carousing went; I hadn't got down to any serious debauchery. The police, yes, perhaps. Or did you think to try the hospital? No? Well, I was intent on getting up here, so neither did I. But we go through Anse Lima; I'll ring from a kiosk there.'

But the casualty ward had only the

occasional punched nose and small fracture to report; nothing from farther afield than the town. When he returned to the car, presently Elyot asked, 'How is it you weren't doing the party round yourself with Brandon?'

'He didn't ask me. We aren't—exactly—speaking.'

'No? Sounds childish, that. Since when? Or needn't one ask?'

Donna said uncomfortably, 'I'm sure you know. Bran didn't like the home truths I came out with that night. But they had to be said.'

'On the evidence you thought you had against all of us?'

'On the evidence you'd all admitted to,' she retorted with spirit.

'On which you set up as prosecuting counsel, judge, jury, the lot. Though you could have allowed your cousin the point he made for the defence—that the end sometimes justifies the means.'

'That's just a cynic's excuse! The thing people always say when in their hearts they know they're in the wrong, or are being shabby at least. And in my opinion *nothing* justified those means, nothing at all.'

'As you made abundantly clear at the time,' Elyot agreed, paused, then added, 'I was glad.'

'*Glad*?' Utterly surprised by the admission, warmed by it, given hope, she turned to him. 'But I'd trounced you all, and meant to. How *could* you have been glad? Why?'

He threw her a brief glance. 'Because, I suppose, it showed you were prepared to stand by your principles, and one has to admire that.'

Hope died. 'Glad' was a friendly, olive-branch word. 'Admire' was cold, impersonal. She said, 'Oh. You admired my standing up to you, but you didn't agree I was right.'

'The scheme wasn't pursued any further,' he pointed out.

'Only because I'd warned you what would happen to it if it had been!'

'More likely because we weren't in unanimous voice about it.'

'But you were! Mine was the only odd voice out—' Donna broke off and sat forward, peering. 'That—that shape ahead at the roadside—it's Uncle Wilmot's car!'

Elyot nodded and slowed down. 'It's certainly a car.'

'It's his. But it isn't where I expected. Not as far.' She looked about her in bewilderment. 'I don't know this part.'

Elyot stopped, reached for his torch and

went forward. The other car had no lights, showing it had been where it was since before dark. 'The key is in the ignition and it's not locked,' he reported.

'No. Uncle always says someone would have to need a car very badly to steal his.' Elyot got in, switched on, and the engine purred sweetly. He examined the petrol gauge and got out again to turn his torch on the tyres. 'No reason for abandoning it,' he mused, then pointed the beam on a path leading up into the woods. 'That's a well-trodden path, and he may have used it. Come on, let's go!'

He gave her the other torch and led the way up the path, holding back branches and entangled lianas for her. At what seemed a long way into the jungle of giant ferns, wild banana and trees whose tops were invisible in the darkness, the track branched. 'How is your hailing voice?' Elyot halted to ask. 'Or shall I try?'

But only silence answered his prolonged Hallos, and with a 'This one first,' he started off on one branch of the track. 'Needle in a haystack, but one can but try,' he was saying over his shoulder to Donna when he suddenly stopped, directed his torch downward and stooping, picked up something from the path.

231

'Recognise this?'

Donna reached for the square of linen he held from one corner. 'It's a handkerchief!'

'And ten to one it's his. Look—reasonably clean, dry—which means it hasn't been here long enough to be trodden on by any creatures or birds. Come on. We could be right.'

They were. A turn or two in the path further on they were in a small clearing and at the foot of a giant tree, face downward head resting on his arms, lay Wilmot.

'Uncle!' He gave no sign, and Donna's heart beat achingly as they both knelt beside him. 'Is he—is he—?' She choked on the dread word, but Elyot, feeling for a pulse, shook his head.

'No. There's not much more than a flutter, but it's there. Has he any history of heart trouble, do you know?'

'Not that he or Bran have ever mentioned.'

'Lying fairly naturally too—doesn't seem to have broken anything but just collapsed.' Without attempting to move him Elyot examined the inert form, gently touching here, lifting there, and raising each eyelid, turning the beam of his torch on each pupil.

'What is it?' Donna breathed.

He sat back on his heels, pulling at his underlip. 'Don't know for sure—'

'But what do you *think*?'

'Could be—' He paused. 'Can you take this? I've seen a case before, and it could be—snake-bite.'

'Snake-bite? Oh no!'

'M'm. Ever heard of the *fer-de-lance*?'

She nodded, aghast. 'But it's extinct on Laraye. The mongooses you imported accounted for them all!'

Elyot sighed. 'The brochures again! No mosquitoes, no *fer-de-lance*—which means we aren't plagued by them, but the odd few survive.'

'But the bite is quite fatal—there's no hope!'

'Used not to be, but with modern serums used in time, only the very young and the very old are at the greatest risk, and your uncle seems to have been pretty wiry.' He stood up. 'But we're wasting time, and speed is of the essence. We've got to move him, get him down to the car. Will you stay here while I bring up the gear, or do you want to come with me?'

'I'll stay, of course. I couldn't leave him now.'

'Not too scared?'

She suppressed a shudder. 'No. I'll stand, and keep my torch alight and moving all the while. I couldn't bear Uncle to come round and find himself alone—'

'Good girl!' Elyot's hand pressed her shoulder and then he was gone, the nimbus of his torch receding, leaving blackness behind.

Donna tried not to think of how long she might have to wait until he came back, hauling the stretcher and blankets up that hazardous track. The air was very still, but the essential silence of the night was punctuated by the chirr-chirr of the cicadas and the occasional startled shriek of a bird disturbed at roost.

It was impossible not to remember and compare the blissful promise of her first night on the island with this one. What a lurch her personal world had taken since then! And yet—and yet, had she been able to look ahead, would she have chosen a way very different from that which had brought her from there to here? Knowing Elyot, loving him, caring about his approval; drawing closer to Wilmot as she believed she had done; even the challenge of Margot le Conte's hostility—all of it had been experience, and experience was something the wise ones said you must have, or become a cabbage, neither enjoying nor suffering—just being.

So her thoughts churned as she kept on the move, patrolling the small area. Her legs ached and she would have liked to sit by Uncle Wilmot and hold his hand. But the slightly sinister stirrings underfoot kept her going, and at last she heard the louder sounds of Elyot coming back.

His breathing was heavy with effort. 'I've hacked the way clearer as I came up, to make it easier to get the stretcher down. You'll have to manage one end of it, taking your time,' he said.

After that it was all action, though not so difficult nor prolonged an action under his careful guidance. As Wilmot was still unconscious, neither the brandy nor the Thermos were used. But when room had been made for the stretcher on the floor of the car Donna asked, 'What about the other car—Uncle's? I could drive it back behind yours.'

But Elyot would not let her, saying he had to drive fast and he couldn't afford to be concerned about her keeping up. He would send a couple of his men up for the other car in the morning.

At the hospital Donna waited in an anteroom while he went with a doctor and nurse into a cubicle with Wilmot. When he came back he brought with him the contents of Wilmot's pockets and his shoulder-haversack containing some wilting plants which Donna found infinitely pathetic. 'What—?' she asked, her chin trembling.

Elyot said, 'It's as I thought—collapse from snake-bite. They've found the puncture marks on his thigh. They're keeping him in, of course, but they're pretty sure they can pull him through. We were in time, you and I.'

'*You* were in time. I mightn't have contacted Bran for hours, and I could have done nothing without you.' Donna wondered what he would say if she confessed the bitter uncharitable thought she had had while she sat there waiting. *If Uncle Wilmot dies, that will be the problem of Louvet's future solved for him*, and the guilt of having thought it for an instant brought tears of shame to her eyes.

She tried to blink them back, but one or two rolled down her cheeks and she was aware of Elyot's scrutiny as she brushed them away. And then, somehow, he was holding her close, stroking her hair, and as she gained control, patting her shoulder and finally holding both her hands—none of it in the love she craved of him, of course, but in more

236

spontaneous kindness and compassion for the weakness of her tears than she had had from him yet.

As she stood back from him, murmuring, 'I'm sorry—' he released her hands and said, 'You're over-wrought, and no wonder. We must get you home.'

'Yes.' But the thought of the house, empty of Bran and Juno and full of her worry for Wilmot, dismayed her, and as if Elyot read her thought, he said, 'But you aren't going up there alone. I'll take you along to the Allamanda until I can rustle up Brandon from wherever he may be.'

'Oh—not the Allamanda, please,' she begged.

'Why not? If I can't track Brandon, it's where he will eventually show up.'

'Yes, but—'

'But!' he echoed, his tone impatient now. 'The Allamanda is a public place; you don't have to regard it as forbidden ground, just because you chose to walk out on Margot for the flimsiest of trumped-up reasons—'

Donna gasped. 'I gave her notice by letter, *and* adequate reasons,' she claimed, though realising too late that Elyot would have heard Margot's distorted version of why she had left. She hadn't convinced Margot that

Melford Drinan had meant nothing serious to her life, and Margot had made petty capital out of that omission by telling Elyot that under cover of 'trumped-up' reasons, she had resigned from the job out of pique at her failure with Melford. And now Elyot confirmed her guess by saying, 'Well, Margot felt you had behaved rather shabbily for reasons which she was pretty sure weren't genuine. But that's water under the bridge and your private quarrel is no excuse for your not making use of the Allamanda tonight. So come along, don't make difficulties. You're not going back to Louvet until Brandon goes with you.'

They were back where they started—he with no tolerance of empty qualms; she with no more than nuisance value to him. Their shared ordeal had bridged the rift between them, but even his compassion for her tears had been no more than kindness, the comforting 'There, there!' he might have offered to a frightened child. Donna's depression was complete.

★　　★　　★

In fact Bran had been at the hotel when they arrived, and he and Donna had gone back to the hospital before returning to Louvet in his mini-moke. Juno was already there, having shared a taxi with her cousins, who had gone on to Marquise before Juno had found the house inexplicably empty and had suffered a crisis of nerves in consequence.

'Me, I say to me—Missus Donna still at Carnival wid her beaux. But where Mister, dis hour of night? Tell you, young Mister and Missus Donna—till you come, feel good f'nothing; like no more dan cent's worth ice melting in de sun,' she had declared, and had listened in dramatic, exclamatory horror to Donna's story and Elyot's part in it before she had pronounced the unarguable truth that, 'Fact, don't know who your friends are, till you got trouble. The Mister, he say he got no friends, least all Mister Vance. But who run, like Good Samaritan in Bible, when he in need o' help? Maybe now Mister listen when I tell him Mister Vance good, kind— But maybe not,' she had concluded resignedly. 'Maybe take more dan old man snake t'make Mister Wilmot change him spots.'

But though Donna agreed as to the improbability of Wilmot's change of heart towards Elyot, certainly his misfortune proved that he had more friends and people

239

concerned for him than he would have claimed. During the days he was in hospital he professed indifference to inquiries made about him, but after he came home he was reasonably gracious with callers who dropped in. Donna suspected, though she was sure he would have denied it, that he was touched by the attention his accident had caused.

Their common worry for him forced Donna and Bran to bury the hatchet of their quarrel, and Madame Hué made opportunity from Wilmot's convalescence to assume tacitly that whatever had been amiss between her and Donna was now happily resolved. She arrived, unannounced and bearing gifts, as she had done before their rift, and Donna had no choice but to welcome her, and to speed her parting tactfully when Wilmot, her captive victim, showed irritable signs of speeding her brusquely himself.

In fact, it was she who surprised Donna by telling her that Elyot was one of the few people whom Wilmot had received in his room while he was in hospital. Donna realised that Elyot would have telephoned or called to ask about him, but that they had met at Wilmot's invitation was news to her.

'Uncle hasn't told me or Bran about it. How do you know?' she asked.

'From Elyot.'

'Elyot called at the hospital, and Uncle asked him to his room—just like that?'

'Well, considering Elyot had saved his life, should Wilmot have done less? But it wasn't quite like that,' Irma admitted. 'Elyot asked to see him, and Wilmot agreed.'

'*Well*—!' Donna breathed. 'What did they say to each other? Did they manage to part amiably for once? Or did the sparks fly?'

'Elyot wasn't telling, except that he had put a business proposition to Wilmot, which Wilmot—'

'Tch!' Donna's exclamation was in utter distaste. 'Surely not *another* one, and Uncle still in hospital? What was it this time? An outright cash offer for Louvet? Or another devious scheme of Elyot's own; one that didn't need partners to help it on its way?'

Irma had the grace to look abashed. 'I thought you had forgiven and forgotten all that,' she said plaintively. 'And you did not allow me to finish—whatever was Elyot's suggestion to Wilmot, he did not turn it down, and they parted, Elyot said, with it left on the table between them. Wilmot allowed that he might be willing to discuss it again.'

'Then it couldn't have been anything to do with Louvet,' Donna decided. 'Uncle has

241

always been quite adamant that he would never parley with Elyot over that.'

'But that would be before he had to owe Elyot his life, and might one not think that should make for a little charity between the worst of enemies?' Irma queried with reason, though Donna doubted whether either charity or gratitude stood much chance against Wilmot's deep-rooted jealousy of Elyot and his stubborn pride.

All the same her curiosity drove her to lead up to the subject of Elyot's proposal by asking Wilmot what, when she returned to England, she could tell her father about the future of Louvet.

'You must tell him that I see no more success for it in the immediate future than it has had for a long time,' Wilmot replied unhelpfully.

'But you wouldn't consider its being put up for sale?'

'On the open market—definitely no. In any case, it would have little value there in its present condition.'

'Though Bran says Mr Vance would be willing to buy it from you at any time as it stands,' Donna ventured.

'Vance, yes.' As Wilmot showed no sign of enlarging on that Donna tried again.

'Has he said anything directly to you about it?' she asked.

She got no answer to that. Wilmot said, 'Is Bran about? If so, call him, will you? I haven't spoken to him yet about this matter, but you should both hear it now.'

Bran came. 'Breakthrough at last? Dad has decided to sell to Elyot privately? Well, what d'you know? And what price now all your virtuous dudgeon over our scheme to get him to do just that, young Donna?' he had said to Donna's hasty summons. But the shape which Elyot's proposition had taken was a surprise to them both.

Wilmot said stiltedly, 'You'll have realised of course that as soon as I recovered, I asked my doctor to carry my thanks to Elyot Vance for his help on the night of my accident. And when he asked to see me we found ourselves on—er—tolerable terms. He congratulated me on my escape; I thanked him again for giving Donna and myself such prompt and expert help. He made light of it—said he was only standing in for you, Bran, and that you would have done as much.'

'I doubt if I'd have rumbled snake-bite as surely as he did,' put in Bran modestly.

'Yes, well, that's as may be,' Wilmot allowed. 'But from there he and I chatted a little, and in the course of talking it came out that he has the ear of the Government on certain of its plans, and that he had volunteered to sound me about them.'

'Plans, Uncle? Plans for what?' asked Donna.

Wilmot's rare smile lifted one corner of his mouth as he turned to her. 'Oddly,' he said, 'for a long-cherished ambition of my own— the laying out of a natural park of Caribbean flora and silviculture on a suitable area of the rain-forest. The Legislative Council, Vance said, would appreciate my advice as to the best site for such a scheme and would be prepared to ask me to draw up plans for it and, once it was in being, to act as its curator.'

'Oh, Uncle, how marvellous for you! And you could? You would?' urged Donna.

'Plan it? Of course. I've had my own ideas and plans for such a reserve for a very long time, as I think I've told you. Soubion would be the ideal area, and Vance agreed.'

'And the Council would allow you to plan it to be as wild and rambling as you like?'

'I have no intention,' said Wilmot loftily, 'of co-operating on anything which would approximate to a municipal park. They can accept my plans, or they must employeur someone else.'

Bran nodded. 'No bandstand, no clock golf, no miniature lake, no Teas. Sounds just what the doctor ordered for you, Dad. I suppose the Council would put up all the cash, the labour and so on?'

'I understand so. As a tourist attraction they would see the cost as well spent.'

'And the curator bit? Would you take on that?'

There was a moment's silence. Then Wilmot said, 'Provided I weren't also saddled with the trouble and worry of Louvet, yes.'

Both Bran and Donna suppressed gasps. 'You would consider selling it, then?' asked Bran.

'If I took the job as curator of the reserve, I should make Louvet the responsibility of the Company, to deal with it as they think best. If they wish to sell, that must be their decision. Or if they decide to buy me out of my share in it, that's their affair too.' Wilmot fixed his son with a steely glance. 'You realise, I daresay, that there may be no place for you in the Council's nature reserve scheme?'

'Is that a threat or a promise? Either way, it's O.K. with me,' returned Bran gaily. 'You go cosset your trees and your flowers, Dad, and leave me free, without a bad conscience, to do my own thing. In fact, I'm thinking of asking the bank for a loan to set up my own car-hire and guide firm any day now.'

'Leaving the Allamanda and going into competition with Margot le Conte?' asked Donna, surprised. 'She won't like that, will she?'

'And am I harrowed by Margot's troubles? Anyway, she's too big a fish with too many irons in the fire to worry about the competition of small fry like me—*if* I may mix my metaphors,' Bran retorted, and turned to his father as Wilmot was about to leave. 'Thanks for putting us in the picture, Dad. And keep us posted from here out, won't you?' he said.

Wilmot nodded. 'Anything I learn or decide myself, you shall both hear all in good time,' he promised, and paused. 'It occurs to me, niece,' he added, addressing Donna, 'that it might make for goodwill and show good manners if we invited Elyot Vance to dine with us sometime. Perhaps you would see to it, would you?'

When he had gone, Bran and Donna looked at each other, shook their heads in bewilderment and laughed aloud.

Bran exploded, '*He* won't sell to Elyot, but

the Company can, if it likes! Of all the arrant side-stepping get-outs I ever saw—!'

And Donna said, 'Bless him for saving his face as gracefully as he managed to. He's a polished diplomat, that's what. And do you think he really meant what he said about welcoming Elyot to dinner?'

'Perhaps you'd better invite Elyot and see,' advised Bran.

CHAPTER TEN

It seemed to Donna that Wilmot's hatchet-burying overture should properly come as a man-to-man invitation from him to Elyot—a casual, 'Drop by for drinks and take a bite with us one evening' approach. But when Wilmot declined to be a party to anything so informal she realised such hail-fellow terms were beneath his dignity. Elyot's summons to dine at Louvet had all the makings of a royal command and as such, must be issued by its hostess, if not by gilt-edge card marked R.S.V.P., at least for a definite date and time at due notice to all concerned.

But when Donna, co-operative but diffident, telephoned Marquise to suggest an evening, it was to hear that Elyot was in Barbados on business, and before the day when Choc expected his return, Irma Hué, that human gossip column, came over from Mousquetaire with some astonishing news, of which even Bran knew nothing. Margot le Conte had sold the Allamanda to an American syndicate and was in process of buying an even more de-luxe hotel in Barbados!

Barbados? Donna suffered a jealous pang. 'I suppose that's why Elyot Vance is down there now?' she hazarded.

'Is he?' queried Irma, interested. 'Well, so is Margot too, one hears. So it could be more than coincidence—their both being there, I mean. Though I did understand—and from an *entirely* reliable source—that the new venture was solely Margot's own baby. She'll be moving to Barbados to run it, of course; which would make any kind of partnership with Elyot rather difficult, as obviously he won't be leaving Marquise. No, I think you can take it there's nothing like that between them. Elyot isn't the man to take on any deal in which he didn't own fifty-one per cent of the shares, and Margot's not the woman to be content with forty-nine,' Irma decided to her own evident satisfaction, though without convincing Donna, who demurred, 'But they do have some kind of a business relationship now. I've heard them refer to it. And doesn't everyone suppose they are going to marry some time? And if that isn't going into partnership together, what is?'

Irma smiled indulgently and patted Donna's hand. 'You have ideals, child, and rightly so. But with two sophisticates like Margot le Conte and Elyot Vance, it is a different story. When they marry—if, after all this time of keeping us guessing, they ever come to terms agreeable to them both—it could well be no more than a business affair, with the shares arranged as I have said.'

Needing to turn the knife in her own wound, Donna said, 'So Bran told me about them a long time ago—when I'd only met Elyot once, and Margot not at all. "Two of a kind", he called them, and it seems he was right.'

'And the truth makes you sad for them? For Margot most? Or for Elyot?'

Donna felt her colour rise. 'For—for the kind of marriage it sounds as if it would be,' she evaded. 'Cold-blooded. Mercenary.'

'H'm,' said Irma non-committally, and changed the subject to ask if it were true that Wilmot was to free himself of Louvet without

249

loss of face.

It was both refreshing and revealing to tell Irma something she didn't already know and to follow her train of thought at the news.

She basked visibly. 'Once free of that millstone, you will see the difference in him,' she claimed happily. 'He will lose ten years of his age, gain a new outlook. Saddled with Louvet, naturally as a man of honour he has not felt himself free to consider marriage again. He has been too modest for too long. But now one can hope he will realise that, without loss of loyalty to a first wife, it is good and intended for a man to share his life with a second—a helpmate for what need be no more than his middle years. Yes indeed, he should begin to see the worth of a wife to him,' she nodded in conclusion, and departed, leaving Donna to speculate on how far Wilmot's change of circumstances might persuade him towards marriage, or whether Irma, faint but pursuing, might have to propose to him herself.

Donna did not see her nor hear from her again until she rang up with an invitation to join her for dinner that evening. It would be a cold meal, as she had given her couple the night off. So Irma would be alone and would appreciate Donna's company for a chat. So much was happening to people within their circle lately that it was both amusing and important to keep abreast of what was going on, was it not? Say seven o'clock, then? That would suit Donna, yes? Donna said it would, provided Wilmot would lend his car, and Irma said 'Good. I shall expect you, dear,' and rang off.

Donna was punctual. She parked the car, expecting to find Irma awaiting her on the back verandah of the house, but though drinks were ready there and the table in the dining-room was set with places for two, Irma was nowhere in the house, nor in the garden, which Donna searched, singing out news of her arrival.

Puzzled, she wandered back to the house. Irma *had* meant this evening, hadn't she? And the welcoming drinks and set table bore this out. So where was she? The vintage tourer was not in the car-port which served it as a garage, so Irma must have taken it somewhere, though Donna would have expected her to leave a message, telling her guest where.

Then Donna saw the note. White envelope against white-painted verandah table, it had escaped her notice until now. It seemed to have been penned in a hurry and was only

251

vaguely explanatory.

'So sorry, *chérie*. Called away. A sick friend—you know how one is obliged to answer such appeals. If I am not back to greet you, promise me to wait just half an hour for me, will you? There are drinks ready, and if you feel inclined to wait longer and need your dinner, the meal I planned is in the refrigerator. If nothing happens and I don't get back, still allow me that half-hour of grace, won't you?'

Not much enlightened as to whether Irma hoped to get back reasonably soon or not, Donna re-read the message after dropping ice into a tumbler and pouring herself a lime squash.

'If nothing happens?' Why, what should? Irma must surely have meant to write 'If something happens'—to prevent her return before Donna left. Then that repeated plea for half an hour's grace—why so definite a period? And did Irma really expect her guest to plunder the larder and munch through a meal alone, just because her hostess had been called away?

Giving it up, Donna glanced at her watch and stretched out on a sun-lounger to enjoy her drink and watch the scarlet ball of the sun go down.

At the sound of a car climbing the long drive to the house, she sat up abruptly and scrambled to her feet, ready to greet Irma when she arrived, well within the promised half-hour. But Irma would have brought her car straight into the car-port; this car had stopped on the front drive as a visitor's might, and after a minute or two, round the side of the house came its driver—Elyot.

Donna stared at him. 'Oh—I thought you were in Barbados,' she said. 'Did you want to see Madame Hué? I'm afraid she's out. Was she expecting you?'

He nodded. 'In a manner of speaking, yes. Seven-fifteen precisely, she said, and not after seven-thirty at my peril. But I knew she wasn't to be here.' He eyed the array of glasses, ice-tub and bottles. 'Do you suppose she would have offered me a drink? I see you have one. What do you recommend?'

Donna ignored this appeal as she worked on the enigma of the rest. 'I don't understand,' she said. 'Why should Irma have invited you at an exact time for dinner, if she knew she wouldn't be home? Besides, she couldn't have known. She had to leave a note for me—'

Intent on mixing a punch, Elyot said, 'I wasn't invited for dinner, specifically.'

'Then for what, if, as you say, you didn't expect to find Irma here?' Donna demanded.

He used a swizzle-stick and laid it aside. 'Ah, but Irma had promised that though she wouldn't be here herself, someone would be,' he said.

Donna's heart thudded. 'Someone? Who?'

'You,' he said. And then gently, indulgently, 'As if you couldn't guess—!'

Her protest came staccato, a little shrill. 'I couldn't! I didn't! Irma said in her note—! Anyhow, *why*?'

He left his own drink on the table, came over to her, took her glass from her nerveless fingers and urged her into a chair, drawing up one beside her.

'Because—want to know?—we've been saying no to each other for too long, and it's taken a Meddlesome Mattie of an Irma Hué to put us in the way of saying yes and *yes* and again yes,' he told her.

'What do you mean—yes?'

His hand, which somehow was holding one of hers, shook it gently. 'Come,' he said. 'According to Irma, though she could be wrong, you've been saying it to me for quite some time. And I, without needing her to tell me so, for a lot longer than that.'

'You've been saying Yes to what?'

254

'To the inevitable. To a truth I couldn't believe at first—that I'd fallen for you, my lovely, prickles and thin-skinned dudgeon and all. That I wanted you, want you, shall always want you. That I needed to tell you so; *must* tell you some time, or better still, show you—Almost got around to it more than once. But always, always you dodged away, kept me at arm's length, flaunted your affair with Melford Drinan at me, and finally laid about me with a barbed tongue, the night of that foursome at Marquise with Irma and Brandon. Though oddly,' he paused to play with the fingers of the hand he held, 'it took Irma to give me a ray of hope that same night, after you'd swept out, that you might be saying yes to me too. *Were* you? Had you already? Was Irma right?'

Donna answered that indirectly. 'You say Irma—knew? How?'

'Women's topsy-turvy reasoning, I guess. She said that only a girl who was deeply in love, only to believe she had discovered her idol's feet of clay, could possibly scourge a man with words as you did me. It was your disillusion talking, Irma said; your betrayed faith, your caring—' He stopped short, his grip on Donna's hand tightening. 'You said—just now—I mean, you asked me how

Irma knew! Then it *is* true? No, don't look away. Face me. There *was* something for Irma to know, and the something was—?'

She faced him. 'The same as for you, I think,' she said.

'That you do love me? Since when?'

'I—don't know. It just sort of dawned.'

'For me too.'

'But I had to deny it—because of Margot.'

'Margot! After you had happened along?' He shook his head. 'No way. Though if you hadn't happened, I might have considered Margot. And a huge mistake that would have been, if I'd taken any alliance with her to the point of marriage.'

'But why me?' Donna marvelled. 'I'm plain—'

'You're beautiful.'

'And ordinary.'

'Unique.'

'And touchy and thin-skinned—you said so yourself.'

'And honest. And plain-speaking. And loyal to a fault. And essentially *good*. And sweet and loving with children—'

'How do you know?'

'One has only to see you with them, as I did once with my girls' piccanins at the store. I looked at you that afternoon and thought,

What I'd give to see some of her own and of *my* own at her knee! Wishful thinking then; reaching for the moon. But now—' He turned to her then and took her in his arms. His voice coming thickly, he murmured, 'There are other ways than words, my love, to tell you how I worship you. This way, for one—And answer me, if you can. Show me—'

They clung together, allowing touch and smile to express their wonder and gratitude and promise. At first Elyot's kisses were shyly exploratory—the merest brushing of his lips on Donna's cheek and brow and throat, and she was tense within his arms, not quite trusting the miracle...

If rumour about him were true, this must have happened for him many times before—propinquity with a girl, solitude for them, a romantic tropical dusk, flirtation. And yet... and yet—in these modest kisses there *was* supplication, there *was* worship. He was asking, not demanding her response as his right. Content to wait for it, he was showing her that she was special to him; not any girl, but his girl, his one-and-only—and then, when at last his lips sought hers in passion her response came alive and leaped to answer him in an excitement and desire which matched his.

Now she too was demanding, seeking, sharing delight with him on a mounting tide which engulfed their senses until it broke with Elyot's sudden release of her and his muttered, 'That was too dangerous—the ache of it, the wanting. I had to let you go, or— But you understand?'

'Yes.' She knew what he meant, and treasured the knowing for what it told of the depth of his feeling for her. With any other girl—! She allowed him to draw her down beside him on a wicker seat for two where he said ruefully, 'I'll have to content myself with looking at you, marvelling, wondering why the heck I took so long about it; why I never chanced my arm before.'

'You never showed any signs of wanting to!'

'On the contrary, there were at least two occasions when I made what might be called scouting forays to test the climate.'

Donna blushed, remembering. 'You've always been so brusque with me, impatient of me,' she went on.

'Only with your resistance to me. I'd never been used to that and I didn't take to it willingly. But you can't say I haven't tried to serve you in kind—what about the Dial

House, for instance?'

'The—Dial House?'

'Done up faithfully to period—*your* period as you would have known it before you left Laraye—even to disputed clock in end-gable, because *you* claimed it had been there.'

Donna drew a long breath. 'You did *that* to please me? Oh, darling—!'

'Otherwise I could have patched up its walls, slapped a flat roof on it and pleased my architect instead. Do you realise, my girl, that I had to track down that sun-dial in a mason's yard in Grenada; have it shipped and set it up with my own bare hands? And since we're on the subject of my silent service and forbearance, what about my allowing you to assume I went all the way with Irma's scheme to hoodwink your uncle into selling Louvet, when I could have floored you with a word of denial?'

'Then why didn't you?'

'Because you were enjoying your indignation too much, and it seemed a pity to spoil your fun.'

Donna thought back. 'You did tell me later you admired me for standing up to you.'

'And so I did. It made me like you as well as love you, and liking's just as important in its own way as love. That's the huge difference,' he mused. 'Margot and I have never liked each other—'

'You must have done once!'

Elyot shook his head. 'No, never. There was always this thread of near-rivalry between us; this hostility, her need to score off me and my urge to score off her. I'd give her full marks for business flair, and I've considered more than one financial partnership with her. But we couldn't have built a good marriage on the kind of armed neutrality which was all our personal relationship was.'

'She has always implied it was more than that,' Donna pointed out.

'Again, probably, because she can't bear to have it thought she isn't on top of every situation—in my case, that she could marry me at any time she wanted. And she has always been so sure of herself that I'd have said jealousy was beneath her, until she showed she was jealous of you.'

'Of me? How did she show it?'

'In various ways. Losing no chance to make a snide remark about you. Referring to you as my "little protegée". And once, in a moment of rare candour, admitting that she knew Melford Drinan was engaged all along, and had rather enjoyed your discomfiture when you found out.'

Donna nodded slowly. 'Yes, Bran had heard her boasting of it to Mrs Tours one night, and though I faced her with it, I did my best to help her to deny it. She did, and though I knew Bran couldn't have made it up, I couldn't imagine then why she should resent me, even hate me, as I realised she must.'

'With good reason, sweetheart, once she saw you as a rival. And don't pretend,' Elyot chided, 'that you're 'way above jealousy yourself. *I* can't. I was jealous as hell over Drinan. And you too—over Margot?'

Donna smiled. '"I cannot tell a lie,"' she quoted. 'And so—ever since, I think, the night when I watched you dancing with her in *her* way, and later you taunted me with being a Blue Danube type. But I didn't know why I cared at the time.'

'But now you do?'

'Yes.'

'Then say it. Tell me—'

'I suppose—because even then I'd begun to fall in love with you,' she admitted.

'Then if that was when it began for you, I beat you to it by aeons and leagues,' he triumphed. 'Flowers, theatre tickets, a promise to show you my etchings—tell me, have I ever paid court to you with any of them?'

'Not that I remember.'

'Exactly. Pretty old hat, the lot. But to woo a girl with an aerosol of mosquito-spray, can a man come any more original than that?'

Donna bubbled with laughter. 'You weren't courting me as early as that, so don't pretend you were!'

'And if I weren't, why didn't I leave our allegedly non-existent mosquitoes to do their worst?' Elyot handed her drink back to her and took up his own. 'Anyway, let's finish these, and I'll escort you into dinner on my arm.'

Donna protested, 'But we can't! We must wait for Irma to come back!'

'But she isn't coming back for hours.'

'How do you know?'

'She said so when she gave me my instructions. Told me she was taking herself on the town for a cinema show and supper after it, giving me a clear run with you until midnight, and that dinner would be laid ready for us on the table.'

'Which it is,' Donna confirmed. 'Places laid for two.'

'Well, there you are. Irma didn't mean to play gooseberry as well as matchmaker. She did her bit, and then relied on our self-help.'

'How did she know we would want to eat together? She assumed a lot. And to think I believed her story of a sick friend!'

'Only a very pale grey lie; just an extension of "All's fair—",' Elyot countered. 'Besides, she's probably hoping we shall do as much for her when she steps up her campaign to get Wilmot.'

'I didn't know you knew about that,' Donna said.

'Who could help it—the unfortunate man!'

Donna laughed. 'Does that mean you think she'll win in the end?'

Elyot shrugged. 'I shouldn't like to say. Up to date it's been a case of irresistible force against the immovable object, but once Louvet is off both their backs, they may come to terms.'

Donna tucked her arm into his as he moved towards the house. 'And you'll be taking on Louvet?' she asked.

'Just as soon as your Company will make a deal with me. I can hardly wait,' he said.

They found cups of Vichyssoise soup, a cold fowl, salad and a chocolate mousse in the refrigerator and pretended, at Elyot's suggestion, that they were eating their first meal at Marquise. 'This is how it will be every night, once we're married,' he said. 'You there; I here. But no, not so far away. Near enough to be kissed between courses if I feel so disposed. As I do now, even before we begin.'

Afterwards they debated how they could thank Irma, and decided to leave her a posy, though it had to be of her own flowers. They wandered round the garden in the darkness, gathering some golden allamandas here, long chenille tails there; sprays of pink crape myrtle, short-lived hibiscus, with a cluster of passion flowers for the heart of the posy. Donna arranged it deftly and they left it at the base of a table-lamp where Irma could not fail to see it.

Then they turned out all the lights but that one lamp, and Elyot insisted on driving Donna home in his car. He would return for Wilmot's later.

They talked intermittently on the way— 'Do you remember?' and 'This reminds me of—' and 'Supposing—?' and 'I never thought—'; happy, cosy chat, sure of eager response. When they reached Louvet they took a long time to say goodnight, and when at last Elyot agreed that they must part, he asked idly, 'How did you know I'd gone to Barbados?'

Donna told him.

'So does the breach-bridging invitation to dinner with Uncle-in-law-to-be still stand?' he asked.

'Of course.'

'And what do you suppose he's going to say about Us?'

'Perhaps,' said Donna, 'you'd better come to dinner and see.'

The publishers hope that this
Large Print Book has brought
you pleasurable reading.
Each title is designed to make
the text as easy to see as possible.
G. K. Hall Large Print Books are
available from your library and
your local bookstore. Or you can
receive information on upcoming
and current Large Print Books by
mail and order directly from the
publisher. Just send your name
and address to:

G. K. Hall & Co.
70 Lincoln Street
Boston, Mass. 02111

or call, toll-free:

1–800–343–2806